Liam and Heidi

Liam and Heidi

Jason Alpert

www.jasonalpert.com

Library of Congress Cataloging-in-Publication for this edition:

Liam and Heidi by Jason Alpert

Summary:

After an abortion Liam and Heidi get more than they bargain for, until they learn how to play along.

[1. School-Fiction 2. Sales Career-Fiction 3. Pregnancy-Fiction 4. Death-Fiction]

Front cover is of two people in a handshake.

LCCN 2018967392

We can do it now.

TABLE OF CONTENT

CHAPTER ONE

Heidi

I'm at Ron and Rae's house. They are also known as **the twins.** If you were a senior at Lincoln High School, it's a graduation party. For everyone else, it's the first party of the summer. Their parents aren't home. It's early in the afternoon. I am going into the other room, and I see this boy come in the front door. We crashed into each other in the hall last week. It was simple, really. I could only grin as he handed me the book that I dropped. He takes a quick look across the room. He catches me looking at him. Then, I walk around a wall and into the kitchen.

Everyone is around the kitchen table watching a game of beer pong that's being played. There aren't any empty chairs. So I sit on Kevin Henderson's lap. "You must have passed our trig final, because I saw you get a diploma at graduation," he says.

I was in a musical my senior year. After it had its run, all my time went into turning my school work into passing grades. I made an effort in math class, but I also had Kevin as a tutor. He's a pretty smart guy. "Yeah, look at us celebrating. Two graduates."

Kevin is the twins' next-door neighbor. He has a social life, but it usually involves video gaming. "After Rae invited me to this party, I told her I would stop by if I had a chance," he says.

Kevin is not actually playing. Instead he is mixed into the crowd watching the game. The players are standing. The spectators are calling out every move. I am watching, and learning how to play. The players have added an extra rule. They are playing beer pong flippy cup. The person with the ball wants to throw or bounce it into a cup filled with beer. If the ball lands, the opponent drinks the beer. Right away there is a ball floating in a cup. People point at the player to hold him to the rules. He drinks, until the beer is gone. After, the person sets the empty cup on the edge of the table facing up. The goal is to get the cup into the air and land it facedown. If they can't do it in two attempts, they have to drink another beer. The first person without any cups filled with beer loses the game.

My attention is now back on the boy I saw at the entrance. He has been drawn into the kitchen. He makes his way through the crowd of people around the table and stops. He is standing right behind me watching the game.

"There is a fight outside on the front lawn," Tommy Harris yells. The drinking game immediately breaks up. People run outside to see what's happening.

Kevin says, "Time to go."

As he stands, I slip into the chair and hear the boy behind me. He is repeating, "Uh, hello. Uh, hello?"

Tommy Harris shouts, "The cops are here."

Now it's my turn. I spring up so fast that the back of my legs knocks the chair into the beer bottle the boy is holding. The chair is metal, and the glass breaks. I turn around to look. I can see he is bleeding. Oh my God. "Stay there," I say. I rush to bring him a roll of paper towels. It's his finger. He obviously needs stitches. It's gross. I wet some towels, and he wraps them around the cut. It still bleeds. So he wraps dry towels around his finger. He is trying to absorb the bleeding. His friends have left. Everyone has run, because of the cops. I offer him a ride to the ER, and he nods.

When we get to the car, I open and close the door for him. "Allow me," I say. After I am in the driver's seat, I turn the key. The car starts to run. I didn't expect company. I have been listening to my favorite audiobook. It continues on full volume. The narrator is reading one of the early chapters, until I push the Stop button.

"Is this an artifact from our high school?" the boy asks.

"It's nothing," I answer.

The title of the book can be read from the touchscreen mounted on the dashboard of my car. He reads the title out loud. "*Alpha Cash.*"

I have been using *Alpha Cash* since I was sixteen. The book first went on sale in the summer before my junior year. I found it being advertised on my favorite website. It was exactly the kind of book I was looking for. *Alpha Cash* tells the listener how they can take a sales-focused approach to life.

I smile at him and pull the rearview mirror to me. I just nailed this boy, and I don't want to be a pain. I get a brush out of my purse. I think of his balls as I pull it through my hair. I hope that this is something he likes. It's the least I can do. Well, that, and the ride.

At the ER check-in, they hand him the forms to be filled out. I can see he can't hold onto everything with the bandaged finger. I grab the clipboard and pen. "You probably can't write with that hand, huh?" I ask as we go to sit down. I read the questions out loud, and he is answering. We are meeting for the first time. His name is Liam Dean. He is a year younger than me. He does not currently have any prescriptions. Check. When I get to the insurance question, he doesn't answer. I look up at him. He screws up his face.

"My dad died. I couldn't be on his insurance anymore, right?"

"I don't know." I had my part in this, but he isn't asking for money. I don't offer my savings. That has to last me until I get a job.

"I can use my allowance to pay the bill. Just write cash," he decides.

We are coming from a party, but Liam is not drunk. Still, I understand that he doesn't want to call his mom. I'm sure he will explain almost everything to her later. "The Dean's Dough would be a good name for a band," I tell him as I fill in the blanks.

Liam was trying to talk to me at the party. I want to know what he was going to say, but I catch myself before I can ask. If he knows that I heard him behind me, he might wonder why the chair was pushed into him.

"We have to stop meeting this way," he says.

I narrow my eyes.

"We were in our school's hall. Remember?"

We may have bumped into each other, but no one even yelled out an "ouch." "It's creepy that you were standing behind me at the party," I say.

"Why?" he asks while adjusting the paper towel. The wrap that was applying pressure to his finger cut has loosened, but he is winding it so it's tight. "Is that your boyfriend you were with during the game?"

"Kevin Henderson was in my math class. We studied together."

"So that's not your boyfriend?"

"No."

Some time has passed since Liam handed in the paperwork. Things have become flat. I am sitting in a chair across from him. We have stopped talking. We just look at each other, and then look away. I am trying to size him up. I can't label him right away, but after being together for a couple of hours I think he is studious. I also think he is cute. His finger is getting the lowest priority in triage. We have been here waiting for an hour. The people walking in are called in to see the doctor. A guy with a broken bone is immediately put at the top of the waiting list. A few minutes later he is admitted. I break the silence when I ask, "Are you hungry?"

"Yeah. I guess that's why I'm tired."

We go to the vending machine and buy a few different things. "What are you going to get to drink?" I ask.

"I'll also have the Big Teas."

I'm looking into the machine. "Where did you see that?"

"At the party," he blurts out.

"What? A tease? Is that what you saw?" I ask. I think of the *Alpha Cash* audiobook. My book tells me first to search for my innermost voice. I find the *cashier*. I tell myself that the cash drawer is open for business. Kevin didn't ask for money. I give him my attention. I sat on Kevin's lap in exchange for his tutoring services. This is how I paid him. It was a simple transaction.

"Yep, that's what I saw."

I am riled and say, "Let's just eat our chips."

He shrugs and then tries to open the bag. He can't pinch and pull it apart, because of the wrap. It's not my fault. Well, not exactly. Maybe. He holds the bag out and asks, "Could you just open this for me?"

We eat our salty/sweet snacks. Then the nurse comes to take Liam. He stands and brushes himself off. I try to win his favor. I tell the nurse my contact information and say, "You know what? I'll be your emergency contact. That's pretty solid, isn't it?"

"After the damage?" He's asking a question but doesn't expect an answer. It's rhetorical. Then he adds, "It might just as well be you who carries me across the finish line."

CHAPTER TWO

Liam

Our high school's fall play will be acted out on this Wednesday night. It's opening night. Seth Newman and I waited in line to buy tickets. His girlfriend is in the show. A lot of our friends are part of the show. Gavin Gibbon is my best friend. He is the student lead on our school's audio-visual team. They will be recording the play. Seth and I stop by the dugout before we find seats. It's in the back center of the house. That's where the soundboard is kept. I can see that the audio-visual team has put a camera on top of a tripod. In fact, there are three cameras. Gavin can't find the time to say much more than hello.

Eventually, Seth and I pick two seats nearby.

Heidi Vessel is in the cast. She is wearing a skimpy Greek tunic. I see her right away, but I don't think she would know me. We both go to Lincoln, but she has never been in any of my classes. I actually don't see her again until the next semester. That's when I notice her between fifth and sixth period. We pass each other every day in the hall. We have not met, and are going in opposite directions. At the end of the year we bump into each other as I turn a corner on route to class. She was charging ahead. I didn't have time to move. Her book drops and some papers sail, but no one is hurt. We collect our stuff and exchange a smile. Then she walks away.

On the last day of school, we have only morning classes. I hear that the twins are going to have a party. People are talking about it in the classrooms and the halls. All of my friends are going. After the last bell rings, Mike Dunlop asks, "Do you want to go with us?" He is driving, because he can fit seven people in his van. I decide to go along. Everybody leaves school and goes straight to their house. Heidi is at the party when I get there. She just graduated. I want to share a laugh with her about our meeting in the hall. I have an in, I think. So I walk up to her. While I am trying to get her attention, the cops are breaking up the party. It's chaos. My finger gets cut. She takes me to the ER.

On the drive from the hospital ER to my house, I remember that I am signed up for the summer reading program. I'm not sure if I will be able to hold a book. I take out my phone. I try shifting it from hand to hand. It's easy to hold onto. I say, "It's going to slow me down, but it's only six stitches."

"So that's what's under that bandage," she says.

"What?" I ask.

"A real toughy. A toughster."

That night Heidi came back to my house. It was around eleven o'clock. She threw a tennis ball at my bedroom window. The noise wakes me. I bend the blinds to look through, and see her. She looks at me in the open window. She whispers up to me, "I wanted to know how you were feeling."

"I'll survive," I respond.

"I'm you're in-case-of-emergency contact. You should keep me posted." This makes me smile. She laughs and says, "I should get going." I promise to give her an update on my health. She leaves me with her phone number.

After a week of phone calls and texting, I make plans to see Heidi. It's late in the afternoon, and she has driven over to my house. It's our first date. We are talking in the hall. Mom comes up to us. She asks if we would follow her. We go outside. It's my mom, Heidi, and I standing in the garage. I introduce them to each other. Mom says, "There is going to be a garage sale." Some neighbors are getting together to hock their stuff. Mom has been working on this for a couple of days. She has put all the items she wants to sell into one pile on the garage floor. "Would you please help me bring these things to the sale?" she asks.

After a half hour of work, Heidi and I have loaded my car. I go back inside and tell Mom. She picks up the insulated bottle she has filled with iced coffee and says, "Okay, I'm ready. Let's go down to the Bennetts'." We don't like them. We were two of the first five families to move into this subdivision. That was twelve years ago. The whole neighborhood was under development. Those days have past, and every lot has a house. When Mr. Bennett moved his family into that house, they brought a fifteen-foot power boat. It has not left his driveway. It has a weatherproof cover for protection, but it's a rust bucket.

After my dad died, his sedan got passed down to me. We all get into the car. I drive about five hundred feet and stop. I put the car into reverse and look over my shoulder. I am working on backing it into the driveway. Once I'm parked, I can see there are a few neighbors in the garage. They are setting up tables. Mr. Bennett comes up to my window. It's already open, because of the heat. "Everything for the sale is in the trunk," I say.

From the trunk, I hear, "It's locked." Mr. Bennett shouts, "Give it a pop." Then his son comes into view through the windshield. Owen does not play a school sport, but everyone knows that he is trained in karate. He was in Heidi's graduating class. We look at each other. He has tape over his nose and a black eye. While everyone is emptying the trunk, Heidi, Owen, and I are talking. He explains that he was at the twins' party the other day. While he was there, Pat Leet challenged him to a fight.

"Just for fun?" I ask.

Owen says, "Liam, we could have been arrested. I ran to dodge the cops. I went around a corner and hid behind some bushes. It sucked." It was only a three-minute round, but, then, I remember the chaos the fight caused. I look at the finger I got stitched.

Go figure.

Crazy.

Heidi steps in. "Well, the best is yet to come."

After the car's trunk is empty Heidi and I take off.

From the street I can see Udders written on the outdoor sign. I eat at this cereal bar often. I pull off the road. There is a pack of electric mopeds outside. When we enter the café, it is filled with students. There is one long bar. On the other side, the servers are working at a fast pace. They are pulling cereal from brimming hoppers. They sell sixteen varieties. You can ask for just about any topping.

There is a short wait before we are asked what we want.

Heidi and I have been together for a couple of hours. She is up close for the first time today. I now get a minute to check her out. She is five feet nine inches tall. I know this because she is the same height as me. She is wearing a tight pink tee shirt with sleeves that ride up to her shoulders. Her chest is made up of medium curves. She's looking cute in a pair of capris.

One of the servers becomes free. We order two bowls of cereal. We both get Magic Marshmallow with vitamin D milk. The best. We also order smoothies. The cups and bowls are black-and-white spotted like you see on a cow hide. It's a standard piebald pattern. In the eating area there is a life-size plastic cow. He is standing on his hind legs. Like everything else here, he is white and black and glossy.

After we sit, Heidi explains that she wants to enter the workforce. She asks, "What have you got planned for the days following your high school graduation?"

This coming fall I will become a senior. "I want to graduate. In the long run, I am going to pursue a higher education."

"A lifer?" she asks.

"Pretty much."

"Yeah," she says in approval.

"I thought you would have gone to college just to get experimental with your dorm room roommate," I say. I meant it to be flirty, but it sounds sophomoric. She licks her spoon in a sexy way. She pulls it off.

Tomorrow is Saturday. I have a load of homework. The summer reading program has started. I can still laugh about how I met Heidi. I take my lumps in stride. After our impactful meetings, I decide we can have a few more. I ask Heidi what she is doing on Sunday. She doesn't have plans. I ask her out.

It's about four o'clock on Sunday. I get a call from Mom as I am finishing my homework. She says, "Our neighbors have been working hard to make sales all weekend." It's the last hour of the sale. She asks me to come back to the Bennetts' to pick up what she has not sold.

Once I am there, Owen and I get into another conversation. Owen tells me that he is going to a small college next year. He wants to become a physical education teacher. I guess he's a pretty solid dude. Then my mom walks up to us. Owen lets out a snort. He has been recuperating at his house all weekend. He has the goods on my mother. "Liam," he asks, "did you know your mom brought your Chin Tongue cd's to the sale?"

I love this band. I listen to them on the shelf stereo. Sometimes I make the bass rattle the windows. She must have brought the cd's to the sale on her own. I look at Mom and say, "I did not know that."

Owen has a big laugh. He says, "Yep. They were just about the first thing sold."

Then with Owen, Mr. Bennett, the other sellers, and me waiting, Mom says, "Now if we could just sell that darn boat."

CHAPTER THREE

Heidi

When he was a child, Dad didn't get the best of anything. My grandparents didn't have the money. Dad can get possessive. He's really vocal about how he is the one that pays the bills. My parents rent the house where we are living because Dad goes from job to job. Lincoln is the third high school I have attended. It's in the town of Centerville. When we moved, nothing good came along. I had no friends for some time. It was only my parents in my life. Dad was always around. I could not get enough oxygen. I practically live in hysteria. They didn't want to send me to a psychiatrist.

"The 'authorities' don't always get it right," he says about the shrink.

Instead, Dad bought me a used car. He went over some road rules before he handed me the keys. My parents said they want me to have all of the fresh air in the world. Dad also mentioned that he and Mom are not going into retirement with a cushion in the bank.

See?

When I lived in Hudson, my best friend Leah's mom owned a catering company. It was called Headcleaver's. We were part of her crew. There was a group of us, and we all worked the same parties. We were servers, bussers, and dishwashers. I was scheduled for the few parties she catered each month throughout the year. Soon, it seemed to me that money was easy to get. I began to try to interest one of the boys.

By the time I was in the eighth grade I had developed. The school I went to would have dances. I was fourteen. I was taller than most boys in my grade. That was what would make or break being asked to dance. The people at work were older. At the parties, I would take smoke breaks with the staff. We would talk. They went out on dates. I would listen as they bragged about having sex. I got told that the guy I liked, liked me. The servers explained to him that it was totally cool.

After clearing a table, I would walk everything straight back to the dish room. That's where Keith Corey worked. He altered his uniform. He cut both of the sleeves off. He was slim, but bumpy with muscles. Also, he was eighteen. I would flirt with him—all that I could. In the kitchen, the boys had connected a cell phone to speakers. They would play the radio. I didn't try to talk over the music. Keith's hair and eyes are really dark features. It was nice just to look at him.

When the time came, Keith and I made a date. I let my parents know that I had to work. I told them, "After work, I am going to sleep at Leah's house." Leah knew I had planned to stay with Keith, but told her mom I had a ride home.

We worked a wedding at a country club. The party broke up at around one o'clock. The last few stragglers left the party. Keith closed the kitchen. We went out the back. The moon lit the outside as we walked across the golf course to a shed. Just the entrance was lit. When we walked in, it was dark. The bartender gave him a bottle from the bar. I had some gin. The air smelled like a meadow. My eyes adjusted, and I could soon see inside. A pallet was stacked with bags filled with lawn seed. I sat down. He sat down. When I lay back, it was like I was on a mattress. He had a condom. I wasn't saving myself forever, so I agreed.

After that night, the crew people would pop up from out of nowhere. They would yell out, "Keith." They wanted to know if everything was cool between us. I would always say yes. Any other answer and I would lose the whole crew and their respect. I didn't speak to Keith outside of work. My parents never met him. I only spent the one night with him. Mainly, it was enough that I was working and getting paid. I loved the money. After I finished my freshman year of high school, my family moved. Keith and I don't talk. Also, I lost touch with Leah. A year later we moved again. I started my junior year at the house we are at now.

I walk out the sliding door and onto the patio. Dad works on our pool. The water is crystal clear. There isn't any weeding that needs to be done. Dad, Mom, and I pulled them as soon as the weather turned warm. The patio furniture looks to be in good condition. It's six o'clock at night. Liam is on his way over. Finally, I have someone to entertain at our house.

When Liam knocks on the front door, my dad lets him inside. My parents send him to the pool out back. I wave when I see him. Liam is wearing a tank top and shorts. He is husky and is covered with body hair.

When Dad and Mom come out, Liam is lying on the lounge chair. Mom sits on the chair next to Liam. She is facing him and starts a conversation. "Sorry to hear about your dad," she says. There is a long pause. She is just looking at him. Patiently waiting for a response. Mom didn't go to medical school, but she works in a doctor's office. She does the billing.

"He died and I am still young," Liam says. He has a shake in his throat. "I only knew him for a short time."

"Do you have anyone that you can turn to if you need help?" Dad asks.

"My grandfather Dean and my uncle Dan. They can be called to help out."

Mom says, "It's good to hear that your family is involved with you. Your dad will always be a part of your life."

Dad says, "Well, you take care."

My parents go inside.

I take off some clothes. I strip off my shirt and shoes. I have on a bikini and jean shorts. Wait until you see me wet, I think to myself. I give Liam not one, but three smiles. I'm going to pad my chances. I don't want us to separate this summer.

Bailey

I park in the street and walk up Heidi's driveway. When I am at the top of the drive, I turn around. I look for the twins. They're just a step behind. The stone path I take leads to the gate in the fence. The fence is wood. It surrounds the backyard. After lifting the lock, I hold the door open for the twins. They walk through the threshold and onto the patio.

I hear Heidi yell, "Gatecrashers!"

Heidi's modus operandi? To keep everyone in check.

Ron walks up to Liam and starts off, "Bro, it's a carefree summer. I sleep 'til noon." They fist-bump. Ron puts the case of beer he has brought under a chair and sits down. He looks at Rae and says, "We didn't get a house with a pool."

"Posh suburban lifestyles," says his twin. They are fraternal. One boy. One girl.

Ron will not get in that water. While we were doing the musical, he would try to get our drama teacher to excuse him from gym. He would say things like, "I have to get measured for my costume." He hates to exercise, but it never worked. Am I one to talk? No. I will not get in that pool either. My kinky hair would frizz, and that is something no one wants to see.

"How is my friend Haley?" Liam asks Ron.

"She knew I was graduating and defected," he says solemnly.

Haley Lowell is in Liam's class. She has been dating Ron for two years. This is the first I am hearing about the now ex-girlfriend. It's good to know. I have pined for Ron since we became freshmen. We both did theater. Good old Ronny.

I nod at Liam to credit his fruitful prying. This may be a good summer indeed.

Rae looks at me. "So what is this new source I am hearing about?"

She is asking me about the announcement Lincoln media center just made. "It's our school's thirty-minute talk show. It's called *Walking and Talking*. The host talks about alumni past and students present," I explain.

Ron asks, "Are we supposed to know the people that come onto this show?"

"I think we are going to know some of them. The bio I saw was of a local vet. She saved a horse that fell through the ice on a pond. Doc was in the class of '86."

Rae lets out a deep sigh. "Our lives are so sheltered."

Liam says, "My friend Gavin is always at the media center. He works on that show."

"We've met," I say. Gavin Gibbon covers the theater program, too.

There is a cable channel that the county schools use as an outlet for all of the scheduled events they record each year. *Walking and Talking* plays every month on a Wednesday night. Also, our high school musical aired on this channel. It was a quality production. I applaud Gavin. I want to watch it again, but this time with Heidi.

We planned to do that today. I try to keep every one of us drama kids in the loop.

"We can watch the musical inside. I'll get the cooler and fill it with ice packs," Heidi tells everyone.

When she returns, we have already turned on the television and found the station. All of us have sat down on the sofa. Heidi's parents have gotten comfortable in their bedroom. "Okay, we can dump the beer into the cooler."

I've been doing theater for four years. My sole campaign in high school was theater. I lived and breathed theater. Lincoln puts on a fall play and a spring musical. My senior year I moved from the stage to behind the scenes. I was the stage manager. We first gave Heidi a nonspeaking role in the play. Later, Heidi auditioned for a small role in our spring musical. I was on the panel again. We asked her to put the song and monologue she had prepared to the side. We gave her a new script. She did a cold read. We asked her to sing. Both were good. She had the raw natural talent we needed. She got the lead role.

I can hear the boys talking before we click Play.

"I went to the drive-thru before every show," Ron tells Liam. "Can't perform on an empty stomach."

I say, "And I credit you. You and your vocal cords."

I know Rae doesn't like his diet. She tells us, "He ate chicken bites and mint shakes."

Liam gives a description of the drink and laughs. "They're green. That rules."

We are fifteen minutes into our version of *Weekdays the Musical* as the beers start to roll. We all touch cans. I haven't interacted too much with Liam since we started school. We have both matriculated Centerville schools, but I am a year older than him. I may have seen him around on the playground during recess. I remember the year we had the same lunch hour. He's good with me. He's welcome to hang with us drama kids.

I remember studying the musical on DVD with Heidi and some of the other actors. We cast our show a lot like the original silver screen movie version. Heidi is quite the specimen. She won a loyal fanbase. The house was packed. After the musical has played, I turn to Heidi and say, "Really, a polished performance."

She smiles broadly and says, "I'm the only alpha girl you know."

I look at Rae and say, "Your commitment was questionable."

"Oh, come on," she pleads. "I had school work, but I still went out for extracurriculars."

The twins are going to the same college next year. Ron will be leaving Centerville and moving to the big city. Eventually I will make my move on him. I got a good K-12 education. I want to find a job in the theater. I'll move to the city to do it, too.

CHAPTER FIVE

Liam

In the morning, I call to make plans with Heidi. "My mom is in the hospital. In the afternoon, I am going to visit her," I say.

"She'll love to see you."

"Yeah," I agree. "I'm going to pick you up at seven. We can go back to my house."

"I'll be ready for you," she says.

Heidi is choice.

When I get to the hospital, Mom's lunch was already served. She is done eating. Her tray is set out on a table with wheels. I pull the table close to a chair and adjust the height. I have a fast-food order from the downstairs burger restaurant. I set everything out onto the tabletop and sit down. She asks me about my morning.

"I have been doing some work for my summer reading program," I tell her as I squirt out ketchup onto the wrapper. I drag a fry through and put it into my mouth.

Mom says, "Those fries look good."

"How is the food here?" I ask as I lift the cover off her plate. She had a piece of fish with a side of broccoli. She ate only half.

"They steam everything," she answers.

"French fries aren't on the menu, huh?"

"None. Could I have a few of yours?"

I put some on a napkin and bring them to her.

"You can't eat that stuff. Your diet is restricted." We turn to see who is at the door. It's Uncle Dan. He steps into the room.

I knew eating my meal in front of Mom may cause a craving. Only my day has already been filled with activities. Earlier, I had homework. I am taking a break from the books. I haven't been to visit Mom today, until now. Later, I have plans to see Heidi. I had to combine some of the activities. My uncle Dan will think this is an example of someone with poor time management skills. He has told me for the past year that Mom's cholesterol levels are high. "There are foods she should not be tempted to eat," he says when I bring in an outside meal. That problem is saltine sized. She has cancer.

I've already lost my dad. Memorial is the same hospital where my dad got his primary care. When I was in middle school, Dad got sick. He had cancer in a gland. It isn't easy to treat. I didn't have my driver's license. My older sister, Allison, took me to visit him at the hospital. I remember her telling me matter of factly, "He's going to die." I believed her. At the end of her senior year of high school, she got into a fight with her boyfriend. They broke up. Two months later she left home. She lives on her college campus. She only comes home during the holidays.

"Oh, that reminds me," Mom says, "Jane came to visit." That is Uncle Dan's ex-wife. "Her father wants to know if you are available to work."

Every year Centerville has a Fourth of July fireworks show. The town didn't collect any money, but they paid for the fireworks. It cost them money. The crowd largely used to be made up of city employees. The police and firemen would bring their families. The guys that worked at the courthouse liked to go. It wasn't helping any of the tax-paying business owners. Eventually, a different group got voted into office. The new city council put together new attractions. They moved the fireworks show out of the park and worked it into the downtown. Now the public fills the restaurants and shops. There is adult entertainment. They set up games and rides for the kids. The shows became popular.

Jane's family made kitchen equipment. Her father, Mr. Veld, bought a downtown property. They were going to open a retail store. The rural offices where they assemble the equipment has recently been sold. The Velds are out of the manufacturing business, but they still own the land in town. They never built the store. The lot generates income because people going to the summer events pay to park. I've worked at the lot for the past three summers.

"Didn't Mr. Veld hire Grandpa Dean to sell their property?" I ask Uncle Dan.

"Yes, and eventually it will be sold," he answers.

Mom says, "For now, they want you to come back to work. It sounds like this could be the last time."

I nod and say, "I'll take the job." I'm already getting itchy thinking about the dirt-and-crabgrass lot. I'll be out there in a matter of days trimming. I know that I'll have help. We'll be whacking down weeds. Putting the big rocks into a wheelbarrow and pushing them away. We do this same job every year. It's a lot of work, but everything has to be ready for the season.

The summer has only just begun, and tonight is the night. I'm sure of it. I'm stressed out. I ask myself what I know about sex. I go through a mental list: (a) I think about what I've learned from my school life skills course, and (b) I visit websites where I can look at the ladies. Not much real experience. It's been a long time since I was in the eighth grade and kissed Rori Brooks. When I was a junior, I got together with Shaw Hall. She only let me touch her boobs. What's really important here is that this is something Heidi also wants.

After I ring the bell, Heidi answers her door. Her parents are in the kitchen. Her mom calls out, "Are you sure you are not going to eat dinner with us?"

"No thanks."

"What about Liam? Maybe he is hungry."

Heidi says, "He's not," and closes the door behind her.

We get into my car, and I drive to my house. On the way out of the subdivision, I make a turn onto the twins' street. We are going to drive right past their home. When the police came to the twins' party, they found a house full of students. Many had graduated on that day. The cops had two cars out on the street. They were there to break up the party. They flashed their lights. It didn't take long for everyone to move along. The twins only got a warning, but one of the officers stayed on their street. They did not want anything to get started again. As we drive past their house, Heidi and I both turn our heads to look. Any bottle dropped onto the lawn has been recycled. Any signs of a party removed.

It has gotten dark outside. We are sitting on the couch in my family room. The television is on, but the sound is off. We are kissing. Heidi keeps pressing her palm into my groin. Then we go a little further. She unbuttons my pants and asks, "Is this your first time?"

"Yes." My libido has been active for about four years. It's now wide awake. "You? Is it yours?"

"No, I've been with someone."

I have friends who have already lost their virginity, but I am a little startled. "Oh?"

"It was a while ago. Before we met."

"I guess that's okay," I mumble. I would like it to be a first time for both of us, but I don't think about it too deeply. We go further again. She has given the signal she is ready. I take the blanket off the couch. I put it onto the floor, and we both lie down.

Heidi says, "I've been panicky all day. I knew we might hook up tonight."

"Well you are looking at fifteen to twenty hours of sex education."

"Good. No, that's good."

I'm hoping she can help the situation when I say, "But I don't know what to do right now."

"Yeah. That class has a different focus." She laughs. I'm guided into position. Heidi has given me her full consent. That is what I was after, and it worked. Cool. We're synched. She says, "When the boy is on top of the girl, it's called *missionary*."

Afterward, I make a few gestures of care. Like I stroke her arm. Then we are just lying silently. The only light is from the television, and she says, "My parents are expecting me home. Will you take me to my house before curfew?"

A few days later, Mom comes up to me. I'm reading on the couch. All she says is, "I found the condom." I immediately know Mom is disappointed. She doesn't like the way I am living my life. This confrontation may be Mom telling me no, but when it comes to Heidi, I say yes.

Colleges like to see things like club participation on their applications. That was a blank, until this summer. Mr. Herald, my academic counselor, said to me, "Admission counselors will be looking at what kids do outside of the classroom." I can't make up for the years that I didn't do extracurriculars. I was kind of busy with everything at home. He pointed out some of the programs I could do as a stand-alone. So I picked one. I decide that the summer reading program looks the best. I already have grade level reading skills. I also always wanted to read some of the books on the list.

Ms. Barry runs the Lincoln reading group. She made me feel welcomed. There are three high schools in our town, and we are all signed up for the program. There are about eighteen kids. We meet at the Centerville public library. It's neutral ground.

The whole summer has kind of fallen into a routine. I save the early mornings for reading. Whenever Mom is being treated at the hospital—and she always is, I take the afternoons off to visit her. I see Heidi at least every night. When the reading challenge has come to its end, I realize how fast the past few months have gone by. I am already looking at our first day back to school.

Amy Perry, the librarian, has been in touch with me. She is setting up everything for the end-of-summer reading awards ceremony. I am one of the senior representatives for this program. I have been asked to pick up the trophies that were ordered. When I get to the shop, I see the example trophies on display in the window. Some are waist-high. They were engraved with things like State Champs. The man working has to find the box with the order Amy made. He goes through a door and into the back room. While he is doing that, I look around the store. If you want to buy a varsity letterman jacket, I can see this is the place to come. They also sell things like pom-poms. They carry them in all of the team colors. Every school in our district is represented.

After coming out with a box, the store owner says, "Here we go." He pulls a trophy out. I can see they are small and plastic. This won't stop Amy from handing them out. After he hands me the box of trophies, I put it into my trunk.

Guy, the man that wrote *Alpha Cash*, is on a book tour. He is speaking at the same community library. I made reservations with Amy. When I invited Heidi to hear him speak, she said, "I totally want to go." I'm learning that it's an important book for her. She has been charged for weeks. We will see his presentation tonight. We walk into the library and meet up with Amy. I hand her the box with the reading program prizes and introduce Heidi.

"I saw you perform at the Lincoln spring musical," Amy says.

Heidi nods. "It's an excellent script."

"It's a really fun time. When is your next show?"

"Oh, that was just something for high school. I'm an amateur actress. I think I'll leave it there, you know?"

"Well, good for you. Great job! You left an indelible mark."

Heidi and I take our seats in the auditorium and wait for everything to begin. We soon see Guy in the front of the room. Heidi beams. He is setting up his computer to work with an overhead projector. Guy is wearing blue jeans. His button-down shirt has multicolored stripes. His belt buckle is a dollar sign, and he has strap-on brown leather sandals on his feet.

Guy begins, "I started out selling Boiled Bunny energy drinks." He is talking into a wireless headset. His voice is coming through the auditorium speakers. "The company had their own cooler in each store that sold the brand. I was working from six in the morning until nine or ten at night. I was a runner. I would visit as many stores as I could, always racing the clock. The driving alone took fourteen hours out of the day. My trunk was filled with cans. In the stores, I would shoot the breeze and add the stock to the coolers."

I have had the Boiled Bunny energy drink. It comes in one flavor, one size, and it always costs two dollars. Basically, it's 205 mg of caffeine in a vanilla-flavored liquid.

"Over time I got an office and had other people doing my old job. I became the boss to ten runners. I was a success. That is when I started the book that would become known as *Alpha Cash*." Over the next hour, Guy gives an electronic presentation that spells out his system. When he is done speaking, we get into a line. Heidi is going to ask Guy to sign her program. We meet him. The one word that comes to mind is *peppy*.

When we get outside, the night air is cool. The summer is winding down. I can see Heidi shiver. I put my arm around her back and rub her arm. I don't stop until she is warm. I also offer her the shirt I have tied around my waist.

She asks if I wanna have a no-pants dance.

A month has gone by since Mom was last in the hospital. She is back at Memorial. Mom might not like all of my choices, but my life must go on. Heidi and I go to my house and up to my bedroom. The next morning we wake up and fool around some more. After, we are lying in my bed. Heidi says, "My dad has found some work. He and my mom are going to be moving to the city."

Heidi is not talking about Centerville. I know they are going to the big city. "Really?"

"I will be following them because I am going to start looking for work."

I am just now learning this and say with some surprise, "The city is halfway across the state."

"I know, but there are a bunch of chances there for people my age. I should be able to find a decent job."

If I drive there to see her, it will take a good four hours. I think about the summer. We must have spent the last ninety days together. We played in her pool, worked at a Fourth of July fireworks show, and went to a rock concert. I have seen a lot of her. I am familiar with her.

"School starts this Monday. When are you leaving?" I ask.

"In six days," she answers. "On Wednesday."

CHAPTER SIX

Heidi

Dad is always moving the family. I try not to become **reliant on anyone.** My family has moved to the city. I've lost contact with my friends. This always happens to me. Moving all of the time creates an emotional distance between us. Also, I am a half day away by car. Liam is busy with school, and we've also lost contact.

My junior year I was mostly alone and had time to think. This is what I realized: (a) I am not at my best being a student, and (b) working will bring out my best. I spent the first week here applying for jobs. I was inspired today. I filled out an application at the mall. Now, I am strolling from one floor to the next. All of the stores I like are in this mall. I'm walking and watching the people. Many are carrying an armful of bags. On the top floor, I find a hair salon. I make an appointment. There is an hour wait, but worth it, I think. When I actually do start a job, I want to look good. The girl calls my name, and I sit down in her chair. At the start, my hair has grown out. It needs to be styled. After, I have shoulder length hair. My bangs are cut at an angle. One single chop, and it's goodbye savings. You need mad skills with the scissors. To finish, it's combed to the side.

It's the weekend, but I don't know anybody living in the city. So I am home. I am at the new house, and my parents are doing some cleaning. I hear my dad call me from downstairs. Dad is in construction. He is always swinging the hammer. He is always wearing a hard hat. Today, Dad is doing a home improvement project. It's cramped living at home. I've graduated from high school. It seems strange that I would still follow my parents' policies. The conditions are updated as I age, too. One of them being, "Help your parents around the house, or move."

When I walk into the room they are cleaning, I have entered housekeeping central. I am already looking for an exit. They can see me dragging my feet. "You know the policy. Let's just get started," Dad says.

This is an example of my parents' brand of love, also known as *tough love*. "Okay. Okay."

"We already agreed on the time we would do this work, remember?" Mom asks.

When we moved to Centerville, it was because Dad was hired for a new job. He was the supervisor of a four-story building project. After it was built, it offered commercial rental space. He has three framed pictures of the building in different stages of completion. Mom has taken them out of the moving box. They are sitting in a pile in the TV room. I wipe the pictures with glass cleaner. Dad hangs them on the wall. He adjusts as Mom steps back. She talks out the centering of them onto the wall.

Mom says, "I remember when your job description was carpenter."

"Yeah. That was residential work. I did those one at a time."

"We've come a long way," Mom says proudly.

When I look at the pictures on the wall, I see myself in the last one. The picture on the far right. I am standing in front of the completed building for the ribbon-cutting ceremony. Dad was foreman on the job. We all think the series of photographs is important enough to display.

We have a crap load of DVDs. There is a metal tree to hold them. I'm sticking the discs into the slots. I go through all of the titles. I already know that I'll be at home tonight. I am looking for a movie to watch. Dad and Mom are trying to figure out which way the window in this room is facing. They don't want the television to be hit by the sun's glare. They find a good spot. Dad marks out the wall, installs a bracket, and mounts our flat-screen.

Mom says to me, "We are going to order a video on demand. How does that sound?"

An hour later, we are standing in the basement. They are having a discussion. Dad may do some work down here. It already seems cluttered. There is some exercise equipment. I ask Dad, "Why did you move with this stuff? I don't see you work out."

"I am in better shape than you," he says.

I'm tall like my mom. Dad is taller still. The tan Dad has from working outside has enhanced the lines on his face. They show his age. From the neck down, you can see the muscles on his frame are toned. His stomach is flat.

"Uh-oh," Mom moans.

"Prove it," I challenge.

We end up on our heads in a handstand contest. Dad gets his legs up first. He is using his arms to hold his whole body in the air. His legs are against the wall. It doesn't look like a stable position. When I get my legs up, I keep my head on the floor for balance. We both have our backs to the wall.

Alpha Cash asks me to identify what is important to me and write out a list. This is number three. I want independence—it's something I am fierce about. The only time I can reach Dad is when we compete. I can show him that I am an able body. This is a chance to look at each other eye to eye.

I am using my chest to stay in this position, but my breasts are really tender. I fall back to the floor. I can't control my feelings. After I lose, I throw a tantrum.

"You two always do this during your contests. Let's just be good sports this time," Mom scolds.

"You win. I lose," I whimper.

It's been over a month. My period hasn't come. I'm late. I want to call a girlfriend, but I can't come up with a name. Weeks have gone by, and I haven't talked to any of them. They all live miles away. I'm all alone, again. I'm scared, but I know what to do. I will go to the store and buy a home pregnancy test.

CHAPTER SEVEN

Liam

My dad already was sick for a year before I started my freshman year at Lincoln. After my dad became sick, I turned all of my attention to studying. I hid behind books, but I have always been a good student. Principal Eldwood has known me since the ninth grade. During spirit week, he discovered that I wanted to go to college at his alma mater. We both wore a shirt with the school's logo.

I have had to deal with my parents' illnesses since that day. My dad has died. My mom was diagnosed a year later. She is still getting treatments. Her doctors are working so that she can continue living well. Sometimes she isn't able to get around so well. Today I think I shouldn't leave my mom. I won't go to my dream college in the big city. I'll take classes at a school closer to home.

In the morning, Principal Eldwood asks me how I am doing. I tell him that I am keeping an eye on school.

He laughs. "When I was in school, I had an eye out for the ladies."

"Oh yeah? Sure," I say.

"Ms. Barry says it was a delight to have you on her summer reading program team."

Ten books in one summer. I got a trophy because I did all of the reading. "It was very rewarding."

"This is your year to be a role model. Maybe get that college recommendation."

"Thanks."

"Good luck."

I am seventeen. It is the beginning of my senior year at Lincoln. I am in the hall between first and second period. I am turning my locker combination. Heidi calls my cell phone. We last talked about a month ago. It was just this week that I was thinking about calling her.

"Hey, Liam," she says. "We should talk after they let you out of school for the day."

"I can't. I am going to see my uncle," I say.

I hear, "Okay, then I'll be in touch," before the call is disconnected.

Dad has a younger brother named Dan. I am going to see him today. There has been a lot to learn from my parents' lives. When my dad died, my grandparents lost a son. That is not natural. Grandma said it brought everything into focus. They now have a passion for guiding Allison, cousin Matt, and me.

Uncle Dan is a lawyer. He and my grandfather, Eric Dean, are partners. They run a small law firm. My grandfather, dad, and uncle all got married at twenty-five. Uncle Dan married Jane Veld. So far, her job title has been Mom.

After more than ten years of marriage, Uncle Dan got a divorce.

Jane's grandfather started a business. He manufactured commercial kitchen equipment. Her dad took it over from his father after he died. While he was in his sixties, Mr. Veld ran the company. A couple of years ago he sold the business. Jane didn't want the business sold. What everyone saw was that she would have liked a job at the company. However, she was not readied to work for the company. Never welcomed into the fold.

My mom tells us, "She is always looking for equality." She called her a *wave feminist.* It made Jane feel acknowledged.

After more than ten years of marriage, and at age thirty-seven, she left Uncle Dan. She didn't think there was any equality in their marriage. The cousins let her know what they were feeling. It was practically an intervention.

"He provided for you."

"We had some good years," she would say.

It raised some questions. They asked more. "You're just going to leave him high and dry?"

"I gave him a son."

Uncle Dan was an eligible bachelor for a year. He has a new bride. She is a divorce attorney. She's also had a divorce. His son, Matt, will be starting high school next year. I see him around much of the time. He has been going through a few personal changes since this started.

Since Dad died, Uncle Dan always calls my mom. He wants to know what she might need. One time he went to the post office just to buy her stamps. Owing to his divorce, the topics they discuss have changed. They now like to gossip about the cousins. He also always talks about his ex-wife. Once he came to our house. I overheard him tell Mom something about Jane. He said, "She has started to carry a wallet in her back pocket. Whenever she takes Matt shopping, she pulls it out when it's time to pay."

Uncle Dan told me yesterday to come to his office after school. When I get there, he says, "Follow me." We go into a storage room. "This box has all of the files of my first three years of practice. The rest of these boxes contain other client files."

I can see that his practice has kept him busy.

He goes on. "I want to store the hard copies. Take these boxes to the address on this paper. I will pay you."

CHAPTER EIGHT

Heidi

The home pregnancy tests tell me I'm pregnant. If only we were more careful, it would have been easy to mess around with Liam. I have a job now. People my age are out looking for mates. It's complicated, but I have an idea about which way this will go. As of right now, I am certain about two things:

I am a day late.

I am a dollar short.

Damn.

I have a job at the Übertrends in the mall. I got it the first week I moved to the city. The two large monitors at the entrance of the store called out to me. They were playing *Fashion Week*. I watched the models walk the runway. Inside, there are signs advertising the clothing brands we sell. It's neon cheese. I'm talking to Sharon. She is the store manager, single, and in her thirties. She doesn't have any kids. She is always at the store. She works something like eighty hours a week.

Sharon has Li and me helping to secure the merchandise from shoplifters. I don't actually have a person that I would describe as an old friend. I decide that I am going to confide in these people. If I have anyone to talk to, it's the people at work. When my pregnancy becomes public, I don't want to be labeled as some kind of monster. The truth always comes out. It's best if it comes from me. I let them in on my secret.

"My parents like Liam," I say as I pull shirts out of their plastic wrapping. That's how they are shipped. "He was always welcomed at my house."

"I just think that you two had a bad outing," Sharon agrees.

I am unfolding the shirts and putting them on hangers. I say, "I'm pregnant." I start to whine. It stresses the next point I make. "If I tell my parents, they will know-ah that I'm not a virgin-ah."

Sharon smiles at me as she takes the shirts. She is attaching a sensor tag onto each one. "I understand, Heidi."

"I had the sex talk with my parents. It was one big lecture," Li adds to the talk. "My parents have never seen me with a boy. They think I'm gay." She laughs. "They can't be serious."

"I'll be with other young adults. We'll be looking for men," I tell them.

Sharon picks up on me. "There is a lot of peer pressure."

"I'm eighteen. It's my choice." I'm resolute as I break down the empty boxes. They need to be ready for recycling.

After I've gotten out what I needed to say, Li picks up where she left off. "All I do is go to parties and look for boys. Actually, my parents will probably regret not putting an identity chip into me."

Sharon and I turn to look at Li for an explanation.

Li has collected the items already put onto hangers and tagged. She is hooking them onto the sales rack and says, "You know? So they can track me."

What I must do becomes clear. I tell Sharon, "I plan on moving out of their house."

"Yeah?" Sharon searches my face. "Okay."

She is complicit.

I go out for some air on my break. I know Tina because she works at a kiosk in the mall. She has a pack of cigarettes. She bought them before going to the clubs last night. She gives me one, and I smoke. In my mind, I go over my options. Raise the kid? We are young and would need help. Liam's dad has died. His mom is sick. I don't think that is fair for anyone. I take a drag. Adoption? I heard that giving up a kid was hard. Abortion? I don't believe this blob can live outside of my womb. I put the cigarette out on the wall and flick the butt away.

Liam may be a possibility, but I didn't expect a baby this early.

I have been working on my job experience. That's what's important.

It's late when I get home. Once I am inside, I find my parents in the TV room. I walk in front of the flat-screen and say, "I'm moving out."

Dad looks at me. He tells me to look them in the eye and give a firm handshake.

I try to keep myself together when I say, "Yeah." I hope they can't read the word *pregnant* that I practically have written across my face.

Mom asks, "Where are you going?"

"With some friends. We're going to find a place."

Mom turns toward Dad and says, "You did it alone when you were eighteen. What do you think?"

Dad nods his head and says, "Good deal."

"Yeah," I repeat.

So far, so good.

On my way out of the room Mom says, "There is pizza." I open the fridge and pull out the pizza box. It's from Daddio's. I love their sauce. I think I will cash in on my 'rents one last time. The pizza is half meat, but I only want a slice of the veggie. I take a bite, but it doesn't taste the same. I know that I no longer have my parents' trust. If I knew that it could so easily be taken, I would have snapped on a sensor tag.

I am at a loss.

CHAPTER NINE

Liam

It has been over a month since I last saw Heidi. She has called and is just going on and on. I am trying to make sense of our conversation. I've missed cues. We have a communication gap somewhere.

I exhale and ask, "Would you tell me from the beginning?"

"I've taken an HPT," she says.

"What's an HPT?"

"It's a pregnancy test, Liam." The only thing she leaves out is the "duh."

"Well, is it for sure. Maybe the lines or whatever couldn't exactly be read."

"It's simple. It has drawings to show you how it's done. I bought a multi-pack to confirm." Then she moves on. "We are RU486. Get it? Ready to cancel."

She's pregnant. Her admission makes us both liable. I pause. I remember when Heidi went on the pill, because she told me. She said, "I had a talk with my mom about boys. My doctor wrote me a prescription for birth control."

We were together that last week before she moved. School had started. Heidi was getting ready for her move. We were just going through the motions. The truth is that I wanted her consent. Maybe instead I should have questioned her on contraceptives each time. It seems that it's the girl, though, that really ought to be more careful with her body.

"When I left for the city, I knew that I would be moving hours away from you," she says. The conversation goes a new way. "You may not even be equipped," she tables.

We weren't doing much different from our peers. What else do I know? Think. Think. Think. "What about our life skills class at school?"

"They don't teach us how to raise babies and pay the bills. School was all menstruation and ejaculation," she says. "We're way beyond all of those things." Then she continues, "Okay, do you have a job?"

"No," I say. She knows this, but I think she is just trying to get some ground here.

"You are not financially stable." She has a very serious tone.

"No."

"Don't worry, I have resources. I will be able to pull together funds."

I'm not sure what Heidi wants, but isn't this a female decision? "What are you going to do?" I ask. I could have been more supportive. I know I just fumbled. Shit.

"Never mind, Liam. Let me call you back." Then the phone goes dead.

I'm beside myself.

After Heidi's call, I think of the Fourth of July we worked together this past summer. Mr. Veld had hired my cousin Matt, his friend Braeden, Heidi, and me. We were employed to park cars on his lot. I was part of the original crew and knew the job. We met early in the day. I took the padlock off the booth and pulled out an old golf bag full of stakes. Every several feet I drove one into the ground. Matt fastened yellow tape around the stake head. He wrapped it a couple of times and pulled it to the next stake. We were creating a barrier around the perimeter of the lot.

I got background on Braeden before he joined the team. Matt told me how Braeden was a skateboarder. In fact, a legendary skater. He once skated his way around the parking lot of a grocery store while digging his key into the parked cars.

"Uncle Dan recommended you for this job," I tell Braeden.

"You aren't old enough, but drink beer." He says hotly.

Heidi said, "you're a key job. You haven't exactly won our respect."

Oooh. Well played.

We left two sections open. This would make the lanes where the cars would enter and exit. Heidi and I were inside a booth. It was not very sophisticated. It had a front and back window with open sides. She was collecting the fee. I was writing it down. There wasn't much space for the two of us inside the booth. She had to turn to deposit the money into a bag. Every time her scent lifted into the air.

A steady line of five or six cars formed in the street. Heidi and I had to keep the cars in line inching into the lot. This was my fourth year on the job. I remembered all of the faces. A lot of them waved. Some even asked, "How's it going?"

From the window, I could see Matt and Braeden running around in their reflective vests. Centerville's city council president drove into the lot. They were flagging him into a parking space. Cale Veld and his sister, Jane, go to the same restaurant every July Fourth. The owner was once one of their customers. The city council president also goes to this party. The restaurant has a deck where they all watch the show. The Velds pursued president Donny. They were always working on their business. They wanted to sell their land.

Matt and Braeden removed the Saved sign. The president parked.

City council president Donny handed out tips and asked, "Who is that girl in the booth with Liam?"

Braeden groaned and said, "You don't want to know."

Matt told him, "It's Liam's girlfriend, Heidi."

The lot's location is the best. Whenever there is an event in downtown Centerville, every space is sold. I put a sign out in front of the booth that said Lot Is Full. Drivers read the message and drove away.

I texted Cale, "We don't have any more spaces to sell."

He texted back, "We are on our way."

When Jane and her brother walked up, Cale said, "We are here to collect."

I handed them the purse.

Jane said, "Everyone is talking about the kids in the booth at the party. They say it's 'love and rockets' going on over here."

Matt and Braeden walked over to us. Cale looked at his watch. "Okay. You're off the clock now."

Jane was always fighting for women. She asked her brother, "All of the kids get paid the same, don't they?"

Cale laughed as he wrote out the checks. We settled once he handed them out.

Jane turned to Heidi and said, "We are proud of you. A tax-paying girl will raise the status for all of us girls."

Heidi said, "Right. Of course."

Jane looked at me. "We welcome men, Liam. Would you ever join our group?" She was talking about the wave feminists.

"Equals, right? Men and women. Is that all I have to think?" I asked.

Jane said, "Yes."

The sun was setting. Cale and his sister walked back to the party. It was still early. The show hadn't started. The pickup only took a few minutes. Braeden's mother came to pick him up. Matt went with them. Heidi and I stuck around to make sure everything went smoothly for the customers as they left the lot.

The building next to the lot was tall. Heidi and I climbed the fire escape until we reached the landing. I could watch for problems on the lot from up here. Once the show started, Heidi and I took a seat. She took off her baseball cap and bushied her hair. I forgot all about the customers. I put my arm around her waist. She was dazzling just like the explosions of color filling up the sky. When the last burst was over, we were still cuddling. There was gunpowder in the air. Everything was smoldering.

The night had been dreamlike, and I asked Heidi, "What happened?"

She said, "I don't know."

That entire summer I spent with Heidi was filled with first-time experiences. I'll always remember how nice she smelled. It isn't easy for me just to not have feelings for her.

CHAPTER TEN

Heidi

Dad doesn't know it, but he is right in all kinds of ways. I will make sure that leaving home is "a good deal." I will have to be self-sufficient, I tell myself. I have to prove that I can be on my own. The first thing I am going to do is move out of their house. I already have a paycheck. Soon, I'll have all the proof I need. I'll be on my feet before anybody knows what hit them.

Liam will have a successful high school career and go on to college. I would never stand in the way of his achievement. My cumulative GPA was a high D+. When I was at Lincoln, my grades were always in the "margin of error." I could not go to a lower grade, nor any higher, in math, phys ed., French, and more. I've graduated. I no longer look for the cute boy with his nose in a book. I'm looking for someone who has a job. A guy with the same goals as me. I want someone who is "in it."

Liam and I both have plans.

My job at Übertrends is good because I like the bustle. I used to work about twenty hours a week, but Cole gave me a full-time position. I think he looks out for me. This is my crowd. These are people who are making sales and taking home money. When I am out on the floor, my pulse races.

I talk to Cole at least once during the day. He has come up to me to ask, "How are things going?" Cole is forty. He wears his silky silver hair over his ears. His body is barrel shaped. The rayon clothes he wears are always in solid colors. He seems to already be on the third mile in this business. I feel like I am watching someone with a lot of experience.

"Great," I say. "I'm sure I will have a lot more sales being full time."

It's lunchtime, and the food court is on the other side of the mall. Tina and I are walking to the Coffee House. I can hear murmurs from inside the other stores. They know about the blob in my belly. After a few minutes, it's not just the other clerks speaking. It's also the customers that are shopping. The details of my life have been leaked out to every corner in the mall. On our way to lunch, there is a lady standing right in our path. She tosses some paper into the can and says, "Garbage," as we walk past her.

By the time we're standing in line for Boiled Bunny energy drinks, I remember one of the chapters from *Alpha Cash*. The narrator read about a man who had climbed out a window and was ready to jump. He had to be talked off the ledge. When I listen to the buzz, I don't seem to be in anyone's favor. These people should stop talking before my story is the exact opposite of that man's. No one has anything nice to say. I am being talked onto the ledge.

Tina turns to me and says, "You're screwed."

What's in store for me?

CHAPTER ELEVEN

Liam

My parents picked a tile floor to put in the entrance hall and the kitchen. The rest of the house is carpeted. Mom has been asking me to vacuum the house for the past few days. I haven't gotten to this task because I am stalled out. I've had the situation between Heidi and me on my mind. At this point, this isn't a conversation I can have with other people. Mom showed so much feeling as she asked me to vacuum for the third day, I immediately pulled the vacuum out of our closet. It seemed like she was ready to do the floors herself. She saw me put the vacuum's plug into the wall. She knew I was in gear. That's when she went out to her car and drove away.

After our last conversation, I have given Heidi some time to decide. Of course, if she does want the baby I would say yes. Some colleges have housing for couples. I could become a working student. I must tell this to Heidi. Although, she may not want a baby. We definitely never talked about having kids. I've been listening to the motor of the vacuum as I push and pull it over the floor. It's calming to me. Upon working my way into the last room, I am spent. I wrap the cord around the posts of the vacuum. I know Heidi may not have heard me say, "It is the female's choice," but I swear that is what I am really thinking. I'm counting on her to make a good choice. The one that's best for us both.

It's been a couple of days since I last talked to Heidi. I must have checked my phone one hundred times before she calls back. "Liam," she says, "I am going to have an abortion." I have given her space. I knew she had a choice to make. All I could do is wait and see. I've felt totally isolated, but here she is with the call.

This girl is a real mother.

This girl is a bear.

Grrrrowl.

I freeze for a minute.

"Liam? Are you there?"

I try feeling her out. I ask, "We aren't going to need a hanger, are we? Nothing back alley?"

"I have access to a clinic. It is safe and legal." She sounds extra sore. "I have an appointment next Friday."

"Really?"

"Yes. My parents are going to be out of town. That's why I have put everything off. While they are gone, I can take care of it. Can you be here next Thursday, and then we can go together early in the morning?"

My mom is not feeling so well. If I go to the city, I will miss a couple of days of school. Yet, I agree. I mean, yes. I fight hard through the initial shock and insult of her choice. I say, "Yes." The choice is made. We weren't exactly having sex to propagate. Of course I agree.

I suddenly feel very bearish.

I get to the city on Thursday. I see the new house. The Vessels bought it from a couple expanding their family. They have two kids and are expecting a third. Heidi tells me, "It's the same size in square feet as the old house, but in a different style." Their house in Centerville was a ranch with a pool. This house is a bungalow with three bedrooms. I go into a side door that lets me into a mud room. Everything smells soapy. Her dad has left a pair of yellow work boots on the rug. On the wall there is a hat rack with a trucker cap.

I'm there around lunchtime, but we don't eat. Instead, we go to her room. Then we snuggle under the covers for a while. Heidi says to me, "I'm allowing you to come to the clinic. You have my permission to be counseled."

"You're an excellent mother," I say flatly. I feel hurt.

"Come on. You have academics," she whispers.

"Yes."

At dinner we eat takeout and drink the alcohol left in the refrigerator. Heidi has pasta with a glass of wine. I dip cheese breadsticks into ranch sauce and have a couple of beers. During our dinner, I make a call to Mom. "I'm working on a project with some kids from class. We aren't done. I'm going to stay the night with them."

The next morning I get up extra early. I get ready for the day. I open the bag I brought. It's full of soaps. I brush my teeth. I step into the shower to shampoo my hair.

I pass Heidi in the hall as she heads into the bathroom. We are genial. After I am dressed, I go and look for something to eat. Thirty minutes have passed. Heidi comes into the kitchen. She has on a small baby-blue jacket with letters spelling out Princess across the front. Her pierced belly button is exposed. She also has on matching bottoms and cross-trainer shoes.

I am stopped at the sign at the end of her street. I ask, "Which way?"

When we are on the road, I ask a couple more questions. I have been holding back. I am trying to gauge if this doctor is at all legitimate. "Is the clinic very far?"

"They are in every direction. This one is right outside of the city. It's about an hour away."

"Was it hard to find a clinic?"

"I read that it can be confusing to locate a clinic that will do the medical work. Some of these places only want to set a girl off of that path, you know? They don't want her to have an abortion. The clinic we are going to has a doctor that can perform the procedure."

This doesn't sound so obtuse. This isn't so stupid. We are going to a clinic known to the public as an abortion provider. The doctor's work will be transparent.

"I did some research on the internet." We've basically said the same thing at the same time.

"Yeah?" She asks.

"Well, it seems abortions use to be explained using statistics. That's how it was sold. And now the graphs, charts, even the rates are no longer published."

"It's our governor who has used executive orders to protect abortion access."

"Still, there is only the gestational phase left. Even that number is debatable. It's a whole new game."

"We have to use imagination."

"The book," I say as I'm baffled, "I mean, it's just out the window here."

"There's a tear in the fabric of my life too, Liam."

Before I go further into the math something pops into my brain. I don't have a paycheck. KISS. Keep It Simple Stupid. That acronym crosses my mind. The next word I say will spark the argument. So I don't say more.

"So we are sticking to the plan?" I ask her.

"Yes. We're holding the lamp. Let's just summon the genie."

"Okay." I quickly agree. We are like an arrow heading for the bullseye.

Big Deal. College is my real goal.

Everything is copacetic.

Heidi

I picked a clinic far away. I didn't want to feel the mass of the city on top of me. Instead, I feel it looking over my shoulder. I guess I'm still from suburbia. When I called this clinic, I asked if I could bring Liam. They said yes. They have a counselor that will talk to both of us. I am fixated once we are inside. I'm definitely here with a purpose. At the desk, I tell the person my name. She hands me some forms. After they are filled out, I take them back to the desk. The women looks through the papers. I have given her my insurance information. She asks, "How are you going to pay?"

I came up to the window alone because I am going to pay. I have a job, I'm not paying rent, and I have saved some money. Also, I remember the time that Liam and I went to the ER. He got stitches. He paid the bill without grumbling.

Miraculously I have my own healthcare card to show her. It was important to my mom that I had one. However, paying for college was always out. "I'm going to put this on a credit card," I say as I pull it out of my purse. "Is that okay?"

The woman goes through a list of names of credit cards and says with a smile, "We take them all."

"The counselor is going to come to get us for a meeting," I tell Liam. I sit and look around the room. It's an all-chick staff. It's early in the morning. I'm the first appointment for the day, but there are five other girls in the room. One of them is so young she is with her mother.

After I took the HPT, I went to a clinic in the city. They tested me and confirmed that I was pregnant. I also talked with a counselor. She told me all of my options. I didn't have to think very long. I will have the abortion because it will allow me to work without interruption.

She told me it was all my choice.

Our names are called. We go into the counselor's office. "Inconsistent use of birth control and sexual activity."

She is no-nonsense. She's also correct. "In the course of reproductive rights, first use contraception," she says to me.

I nod.

She looks at Liam. "A condom is the most effective way to stop a pregnancy. You may not necessarily know how to use or be practiced with a condom." The counselor gives Liam a handful of pamphlets on STD's and says, "You'll learn."

Liam takes a cursory look at them. I hear him say, "Scare tactics," under his breath. They take Liam back to the waiting area. He came to the city because I asked him. I decided that he would be enough support, but he has been in an ugly mood.

In private the counselor asks, "Is this what you want?"

At this point, I hope everything will just work itself out. Anyway, it has been a few days since I left the last clinic. I decided Liam's working student idea didn't make a lot of sense for me. Also, there is going to be some fallout when my parents hear. I think of how I would live without a paycheck. That doesn't make sense. I have thought it through and say, "Yes."

A staff member takes me into an examination room. She brings me a gown to change into. It has been eight weeks and six days since I have had my period. It took that long before I could find the opening I needed to come out here. Instead of taking the RU486, I request to have the elective surgery. It just seems easier to do everything at the clinic. To prep, I take three medications. They give me antibiotics, and another medicine that will relax me.

The staff says, "It will be over soon."

The doctor gives a pretty dense monologue before he goes about his business. I listen carefully. He says, "We have learned from a large sample of clinical tests that there are no long-term risks. We do a regular review of new research. This clinic is up to date on medical standards and guidelines. It's one of the safest medical procedures. The results show a high percentage of success."

"So is this little kinky link still on the main chain?" I ask. I'm hoping to hear that I'm not the only person making this choice.

"Sure," he says. "I've had patients travel to this clinic from all over the country."

After the procedure is done, I am walked to the recovery room. Thirty minutes later I'm still under the anesthetic, but I nod when the nurse asks if I am ready to leave.

"I saw the fairy," I say when I see Liam.

My wish is granted.

We make the hour-long drive back to the city. Liam drops me off at my house. He has to be home to drive his mom to an appointment. I'm home alone. I feel some relief. I take a six-pack of LostOff nutrition shakes to my room. I also have a book to read. I change my clothes and get into my bed. I don't fall asleep. I am resting my back on a large pillow that has arms. I have cramps and have been bleeding. I have aftercare instructions. I read that this may happen.

Things are raw and real. I was in the situation because I was encouraged to use my sexuality. I get this from multiple sources. It's once too often. When I want something I use my clothes, my hair, and my makeup. When I give a kiss, it's to fulfill my good girlfriend quota. I have been working hard to increase my Übertrends sales. I use my body. I wear only skintight shirts. On Thursday I made two sales. I can't have a baby bump right now. One reason I had the abortion is that I still will use my feminine wiles. I am not modest. It's how I learned to survive.

Alpha Cash says that I have gone off the rails.

I went to bed on Friday afternoon. I have only gotten up to use the bathroom. Also, I am swallowing acetaminophen with the strawberry-flavored shakes. Yummy, yum. I've been doing anything I can think of to make a fast recovery. Lots of pampering. I heard my parents come home late Sunday night, but I didn't go down to say hello.

CHAPTER THIRTEEN

Liam

From the clinic, I drive straight home. Mom needs a ride to her doctor's appointment. I am right on schedule. When I walk in the door, Mom sees I have an overnight bag. When I talked to her over the phone, I gave her the impression that the sleepover was improvised. Like our school work was getting done on a deadline. The bag has soaps and clothes. No books. It's no problem. I will put it away in my room before Mom gets a look inside.

As I go upstairs I say, "I just want to use the bathroom."

When I come downstairs, I don't see Mom. I call out. No answer. So I walk outside and find her sitting in my car. She is going through the clinic pamphlets that I left on the passenger seat. I have been up and about since this morning. This was before I could see the sun. I effing forgot. Busted! My bag was a hint to Mom that something more than homework had happened. I didn't even know we were taking my sedan. By the time I get into the car, she has constructed the whole deal.

"Well, I was not at any school function. I'm sorry," I say.

"You did this with Heidi?" she asks.

I can forget about the baby. I'm not a daddy. Mom has lost her husband. The idea of her being a grandma is gone. I expect her to have empathy. "Yes. We aborted a pregnancy."

The doctor's office sees patients only three days a week. It is crowded. Mom signs at the desk, and we sit. The chairs are small. We are all packed in together. The man seated next to me is using the armrest. He has practically stuffed me into the chair. I can't move. The office has a fish tank. An older woman is talking about the oncologist. Every person in the room can hear her. She says, "He has fish. So what?"

We both follow a man into the back of the office. Mom is working with the tech. I am just sitting there. He sets her up and leaves. Mom's doctor is giving her a chemo-cocktail treatment. She talks to me about the abortion. "You did not have my permission."

"I'll be eighteen soon enough." I didn't tell my mom because Heidi didn't tell hers. She doesn't want her parents to know. That is one thing we went over. I let her take the lead. Also, Mom let me know that she didn't like me being sexually active. I made the choice to be with Heidi. This doesn't look good for me.

Continuing, she says, "I see you are going to learn things the hard way. It looks like you have made your choice. You are now a student at the school of hard knocks."

I have to fend her off.

"Well I was young, and without life experience." It's only been eight hours since I was at the clinic. Still she can see where I am going. Mom loves anything that is educational. I hit her where it counts. I'm admitting that there is something to learn.

Mom screws up her face. She is skeptical. "I think you should talk to someone. You are going to have to tell it to a doctor."

Today is the kind of day that can break you.

I'm in homeroom before the bell rings. I'm reeling from the past week. Gavin Gibbon is sitting next to me giving a commentary. "Heidi is a ten. She's a force in the world. You didn't close the deal. Like a duck's back, let it slide right off."

"We spent an entire summer together," I explain. "We thought considerably about everything."

Seth is sitting on my left and says about the abortion, "You practically gave her permission."

I think of the concert Heidi and I went to over the summer. I wasn't sure how to get to the venue. It seemed like I was in the middle of nowhere. I felt pressure. At the light, I picked up my phone, but I couldn't turn it on. The battery was dead. Heidi doesn't have a phone. I had been spending money all summer. After paying for the tickets, I was broke. I saw a Superstore on the road. I asked Heidi if she would buy a GPS. I only wanted to use it for that night and said, "We can return it tomorrow."

She said, "I would be the last person in a line for that plan."

Heidi knew I was on the wrong road. "Why?" I ask.

She said, "That's not the right thing to do. I don't like that, okay?"

I made a wrong turn that took us thirty minutes out of the way. We did make it to the arena. As I pulled into a parking space, Heidi asked, "Happy now? You should have gotten directions before we left." Parenting isn't something that has been mapped out and is easy. We are both teenagers. Having a baby would have been a debacle. I already think of the choice Heidi made on the pregnancy as the best choice.

"It was no, okay?" I tell them about the decision Heidi made on having a baby. She didn't want one.

Seth says, "If it was my girlfriend, I wouldn't even take her to the clinic. You can't be so unassuming, Liam." I used to laugh at him because I know his mom packs his lunch. Now I have a different impression. Maybe this guy can exploit his mom's role as a caregiver.

Gavin says, "Well you are both under the gun now. Ever play lotto? It's the best option you have left."

The odds he has given me aren't very good. A lot of people don't think there will be a positive outcome. I tell him to fuck off.

Mr. Soth has already started the class. He stares at me and shakes his head. I'll have to finish with Gavin later. I listen to the lecture. "For the first time, America looked past its land and developed a foreign policy." Mr. Soth teaches my American history class. He doesn't call on the students to answer questions. He fills the hour with one of his lectures. He seems like the kind of guy who always had a lot of enthusiasm for his subject. He really knows the material, and I like his class.

"In 1919, there was a war in Europe," he says. "Americans had to ask, 'How can we keep the peace in the world?'"

It flips the switch. We must fight the war. I am already under attack, and these are my friends and family. There will be more instigators. The abortion has become a weapon they will use against me. I must fight like a soldier. I am at war.

I am zoned into the lesson for the rest of the hour.

CHAPTER FOURTEEN

Heidi

When my mom was five, there was a kitchen fire at her home. Mom's parents were not fully insured. They had to use their savings to pay for a house restoration. My parents cheered when I started my job. My mom went over the importance of health insurance. She went on for a half hour. Without telling her why, I was sold. I know how things can take place for the worse.

My dad says, "When it comes to healthcare, you don't want to be left with the bill."

I didn't want to put the abortion through my mom's insurance company. No way. I don't even want to tell my parents. It's only a matter of time before they know everything. Now I have a job. I'm going to Übertrends to fill out papers to ask for medical benefits. As I walk the mall, there is another stirring of voices. I want to scream, "Step off," but I don't think they will. There is always a troll, now that I have had the procedure. I'm rotten if you were to believe them.

The next day I am at work. Li is with me at the front counter. Nolan walks up to get the mail for Cole. He is the stock boy at Übertrends. He doesn't make it out of the back room much during the day. We are talking about boys. I say to Li, "I've lost contact with whom would be my baby daddy."

I sneak a look at the stock boy. Our eyes meet. Nolan was in earshot and says, "We can't plan for what actually happens in our lives." I hand him the mail. He winks at me before returning to the back.

I think Nolan is right as I stand here. I trace a history of bad choices. I figured one result of having the abortion is that it would help keep my career path clear of barriers. I mean, I can't "show" at work. Cole says we sell trends in sizes youth to XL. Übertrends doesn't sell maternity clothes. We are very trendy. Just like he says. I bought my wardrobe at this store. I'm there to be a model employee. A good example for the customers. Now I'm stuck at the mall because I need a job with health insurance benefits. Likewise, I'm not sure how long it would take to find another employer with all of the buzz surrounding me.

I like my job, but I am using it to learn everything I can about sales. It's a stepping stone. I don't know if I could do it for the next thirty years. The owner of Übertrends, Cole, runs his store helped by a general manager. I don't see Sharon leaving her management position any time soon. That job seems to be filled permanently. The rest of us are plain old sales clerks.

After helping a customer pick some clothes, I say, "I can let you into a dressing room."

The customer rolls her eyes at me. "I know how you like to play. It's always fast and beautiful."

I know she could be talking about the abortion. Having the procedure is not a source of pride for me. People call me a silly girl. People scoff and say, "It's a betrayal." I'm not believed. Alternatively, she could be talking about the clothing designer's style.

I ignore her comment. I say, "This is an essential piece this year."

The customer doesn't try on anything and walks out of the store. I could not keep her in check. I had no control over her. I am having a hard time keeping anyone in check. When we go out to the clubs, I haven't been able to size up the boys. I don't really know what they have hidden in their background. I don't know how I feel about them. My instincts have been whacko since the abortion. I'm glad Cole and Sharon are in the back. I don't want them to see I missed a sale.

I've always had a job. I worked at Headcleaver's catering company. I could go shopping. I spent my money on fashion magazines and clothes. It seems like my talents are something of the past. When I approach a customer, they don't see someone who is a fashion expert. It's not like it was in high school. The people walking the Lincoln halls knew who wore the trendy labels and turned to me. Every day I walk up to our customers, but they have a no-sale look across their faces.

CHAPTER FIFTEEN

Liam

Without knocking, Mom came into my room. She was giving me a warning about how I should conduct myself, but I decided a while ago that I like being with Heidi. I didn't care about the penalty. Now, I am suffering the consequences. Some from Heidi. Some from Mom. From both of them. I have come up short on character. I did not want to hear this lecture from Mom. Full disclosure, I pushed her out of my room. She did not fall down, but she called the cops. I only wanted to put a door between us, but there was much more. I was put behind bars. I spent Sunday night in the city jail.

While in jail I had lots of time to think. Mom is first an educator. She would be the first to tell you that this situation is a teachable moment. I think she is angry about the abortion, and not the push. Somehow, I missed the lesson. I really did not learn anything. Gradually, I came to conclude that I would never push anyone again.

Early on Monday, I am bailed out of jail. I will be dropped off at school. I know Uncle Dan had a divorce. I was not looking forward to the ride. He has become really quick to object to the things people do. I'm not getting what I expected. All he says during the drive is, "You were being held. Now they say you can go."

Lincoln High School's academic advisors have been guiding our futures for three years. The counselors have begun meeting with their senior students. My counselor is on the D's. I get called into his office.

Mr. Herald says, "Your freshman year you made a plan that would take you to college." I did do a lot of school work when I was younger. I did crack the books. I was a very good student. After I got to high school, I got more serious about learning. I studied and completed my homework assignments. Mr. Herald set a course of study for me to follow. He said, "We have to impress the college admissions officers. This is the kind of thing they look for."

"Yes."

"It says here that you have all of the credits you need to be considered a senior. It's been an academic success. You also have something to talk about under extracurriculars. You were in the summer reading program. I think that was a good choice. Now it's time to apply."

Mr. Herald is a trained psychologist. It was school policy to talk to him after my father died. We know each other. I had to tell him about the abortion. "It could bar your acceptance at some schools," he says, but it's a little too late for warnings. He's the only staff member at Lincoln I told. I opened up to him because I am asking for his help. I must make sure that my future is still on track.

"Will you help me with my college admission applications?" I ask. After the abortion, I'm really not sure how to fill them out. I don't know how this works.

Mr. Herald says, "We can work on a strategy. I think our focus is the personal essay."

"Thanks."

The academic counselor puts his hands together, drops them into his lap, and leans forward. "I don't want you to write something dishonest." He lifts his clasped hands. He uses his index fingers to point at me. "The bar is set pretty high, but standards change over time."

I agree to everything and say, "Okay."

"What I want you to do is write the essay and come back to see me."

The counselor's office is adjacent to the principal's office. I am headed out to the classrooms, but Principal Eldwood steps in front of me. He puts both of his hands on my shoulders. He says, "Liam, your counselor has told me that your grades have been good. But I raise the boys at this school to have character." He looks me in the eye and shakes his head. "Our conduct should be the same even when no one is watching. We always do the right things." He has overheard the meeting I just had with the counselor. The students have looked into Eldwood's career. His record is spotless. I have no ammo. I'm in over my head.

I am saved by the bell because it rings to start class. I leave Principal Eldwood thinking that I would not be a good role model. I don't know why he ever thought I would be. I walk into the classroom with a note from my counselor. My chemistry teacher is on the lesson for the day. I had plenty of time to get to class, until I was stopped. I drop the note on his desk. My teacher looks at the clock. Then he gives me the stink eye.

Mr. Soth assigned the class a paper. I wrote about US foreign wars. During my summer reading program, I made friends with a man who left his home country. He was forced to leave during an ongoing war. He shelves books at the library. He gave me an interview. I'm sure I will get a good grade on this assignment. I am in homeroom. Today we are getting our papers back. Mr. Soth walks around the room handing them out. He gives me my paper. I turn the pages looking for the mark. When I handed the paper in the back page was blank. It's now filled with handwriting.

Mr. Herald gave me a guideline for my personal essay. I want to send my college apps out for early acceptance. I think this will enable me to stand my ground with the teachers at Lincoln. That plan will not work. My academic counselor has already been making the rounds. Things are moving swiftly along. The staff at Lincoln know about the abortion. I have not been admitted to any college. When they have their eye on me I kind of wobble. Albeit, what Mr. Soth has written down may be everything I need to know. On the last page of my paper, he has made a note. It reads, "In the coming days you will find that it is your city that will be under siege. Mankind will come by air, land, and sea."

Okay. I am being warned. No one is willing to indulge me. Now I know what to expect. Everyone will hold me accountable.

I am sitting in the kitchen with my books splayed across the table. Uncle Dan has come over to give Mom a shower seat. They are in the next room, and I can hear them talking. Grandpa has found a buyer for Mr. Veld's land parcel. The new city council started the downtown attractions, and the property became important. The city of Centerville wants to own the land. City council president Donny has made an offer.

The Velds think it's centrally located land.

Grandpa is a negotiator. He is going to work out the details of the sale.

Abortions are legal in my state. I am learning just how often this procedure is challenged. Every year a group tries to overturn the decision. I heard about a mom and dad that live only fifty miles away. They were irate that their daughter got an abortion. At first, they didn't have much of a case. The girl was eighteen. Yet a few weeks later—after she had the abortion—she committed suicide. Her parents wrote a letter to our congressman to question the procedure and its laws.

Outside of their township offices, the Centerville city council members canvass the public on abortion. It's been a hot topic across our state since the mom and dad fought. Our representatives, who make the laws, are listening. The state legislature wants to get a feel for the public sentiment on this issue. When Grandpa Dean works with the council, they ask him how I am doing. They remember me because I worked at the parking lot for all of the events in downtown Centerville. Heidi worked at the lot too. They know our history.

After only a short period, I become mixed up in their business.

The council secretary says, "It takes a village."

Council president Donny has got that ball rolling.

CHAPTER SIXTEEN

Heidi

I have been lying in bed for about an hour. I am thinking of Liam. After the clinic, he only pulled into my drive. I shook his hand and said goodbye. He watched me get into my house. He then left to help his mom. I'm not sure if he is angry at me. The thing I did, I may not be able to put it behind me. I know it was a costly mistake. Today, things are going to change. I'm starting my new hours. My schedule this week calls for forty hours of work. I'm listening for any noise my parents might make. Bing. I hear the shower. After they are gone, I go through my morning routine without trouble. I leave my house early enough to make the drive to work. I start my shift at ten.

I leave work at noon on Friday. There is a follow-up appointment for me at the clinic. It has been a week since I was here last. I don't see the doctor. I'm working with one of the technicians. I still have to put on a gown. After a few tests I put my clothes back on and leave. There weren't any complications.

On the sidewalk outside of the clinic, I am stopped by a middle-aged woman. She is making a petition that will fight the threat of new restrictions that could be placed on the clinic. A girl in our state committed suicide. Her parents are claiming that it was the result of an abortion she had. They are fighting Congress to make new laws against the procedure. This lady outside of the clinic says, "Legal abortions are safe abortions." I sign to help her cause. I use a fake name. She gives me a goody bag and says, "Have a nice day."

On the way home, I stop at the Coffee House. I buy a bag of beans and leave. At home I pull into the driveway. There are only two spots in our detached garage. Dad asks me not to park my car inside. So I leave the car in the driveway. I'm parked in front of our garage door. I am just sitting there, until I see the goody bag. I dump it out onto my lap. There is a pin that says Keep Abortions Safe, that I decide to wear. I take my keys out of the ignition and go to the back of the car. There is an I Am Pro-Choice bumper sticker that I slap onto the bumper. On the other side of the bumper, I put on a Keep Abortions Legal sticker.

Inside I grind the beans. I'm going to celebrate my achievement. The pot is brewing as my parents walk in from work. One after the other. I put out three mugs, and the questions begin.

Dad fills up his mug and says, "What is with the parking job?"

I smile at him. Then I fill up a mug and hand it to Mom. She asks, "Are you feeling alright? You have been acting funny."

"What? No. Never better," I answer.

Dad asks, "And those stickers on your car. What are those about?"

He must have pulled up right behind my car. Now they have their eyes on my button. I have been avoiding my parents for weeks. I am running. I didn't put my real name on the petition at the clinic. I am hiding. It's time to talk. I have the soul of a *cashier*. I know that optimism is as good as gold. I am going to talk them down. I make a quick calculation and say, "I had an abortion. It's over. It was very successful."

"What a cheat," Dad says to Mom. She looks over the mug at him.

"Oh yeah? Well you are one to talk. All verved on a robust cup of coffee." I am calling him out, but the attempt to keep him in check quickly fizzles out. He has only ingested some caffeine. He doesn't even think twice about his behavior.

Dad is still talking to Mom. He says, "What about her job? She is not going to like it when her boss has all of the control."

"No. I have the competitive edge," I say positively. At least I will once I have this thing all figured out. The tears are about to fall as I look from Dad to Mom. I decide to take flight, and run to my room.

Later that night, there is a knock at my door. It's my parents. I let them into my room.

"I'm standard bearer of this concern," Dad says.

I spilled the beans in the kitchen, and now Dad is all business. I know he is pushing me out the door. I cut him off. "I'm moving in with some friends. I just need to find a good weekend."

Mom says, "You're eighteen. We think it's fair." She is talking about the eviction.

"It's thee priority," Dad says firmly.

I'm in full survival mode. I think I always have been. Moving all the time. Always trying to make new friends. I've got to move on, again. This time alone.

All I can even really think about right now is a paycheck.

It's very important to me.

CHAPTER SEVENTEEN

Mom Dean

I am at my art therapy class. There are eleven other students here. We are all sitting on stools in front of a long, tall table. All of the people in this room have been to eight classes. That's two sessions. It's what they recommended, because it's enough time to learn the basic pottery skills.

Joselyn says, "Okay, beginners. Great job. I am really starting to see your work."

The first piece I did was a bowl with a lid. I made it on the electric-powered wheel. Today is our last class. I have my apron on and am ready with my box of tools. The teacher sets my new project into place. I get to work. I have been hand-building ten pounds of clay. I tooled the clay into slabs. I have assembled everything into a narrow, tall pyramid.

Liam and I had it out the other day. I am so mad I could kick myself. I was at my doctor's office all week for treatment. I was barely getting around. I asked him to help me. I told him to pick up groceries. He promised he would buy them. On Sunday morning, I was in the kitchen. There wasn't any milk for my coffee. I went to the cupboard for the coffee, but I couldn't find any. That was gone too.

Last week he told me he was doing homework with a couple of friends. Later, I found out that he skipped school. He went to the city to see Heidi. He's come a long way. He may be slipping back. He used to be so decent. I know I need to see his good nature return. We'll just see what his grades look like this semester. That's also what I thought when his father was sick, but he kept up with school. I saw him doing his homework. His grades were where I was most impressed.

Joselyn steps in front of me and says, "This is your best work."

I have had hours of class time. "I think I have the hang of everything," I tell her. I have been working with a stamp and a stencil and say, "I am going to put on the decoration, and the piece will be done."

She says, "After you finish the job, I will fire the piece in the kiln."

After I couldn't find the coffee, I went up to Liam's room. I opened his door. He was still in his bed. I woke him with my voice. I went on for a few minutes. I didn't know what he was going to put into his cereal, or even when he planned on getting out of his bed. He pushed his blanket away and sat on the edge of the mattress. There was an empty beer can on top of his dresser. He's a stinker. I told him, "I want you to straighten out your life. I'm not always going to be here for you." He reached over and pulled a basket full of his dirty clothes to him. He slipped on sweatpants and a sweatshirt. This led me to ask when he was planning on doing the laundry. He got to his feet. I reminded him about the vacuuming. He came up behind me as I was leaving his room. He put both of his hands on my back and shoved me out. Then he shut his door.

This was right after the episode he had with Heidi. No. I won't allow the push. I called the police. Thirty minutes later, I was letting them into my house. An officer stayed in the hall, and another one came into the kitchen. I gave him everything he needed to make a report. Then they both went to Liam's room. I stayed in the kitchen. Ten minutes later, I could hear the front door open and close.

Nobody said a word. Liam was put into the back of the police car and taken to the station.

He is going to learn his lesson.

Josalyn is now in the center of the room. "Everyone. It's break time. See you in fifteen."

I stop at my cubby to get the bottled coffee I brought. I go outside. It's late in October, and the sun is out. I hear some people talking about our first day of class. It's the usual group. No therapist. "I like when we get the clay," I contribute. "When I get my hands wet and I am kneading."

"That's just mud," Jim quibbles. "The front of our aprons and our sleeves are caked. Even my glasses get splattered."

When I twist off the cap on my drink, it clicks. I swallow some and say, "But that's when we get the chance to really whip that lump into shape."

On the way home, I am thinking about my dilemma. Liam's uncle picked him up from the police station on Monday. He thinks Liam should be put on social security disability assistance. Liam agreed to go see the doctor. We'll see what he says.

Liam also made me promise I would give Heidi a chance to tell her parents. She is eighteen years old. I don't make the call to her house.

For now, Liam's back with me at home.

I am conked out.

CHAPTER EIGHTEEN

Liam

As it turns out, the abortion is a no-no for some people. I am at a doctor's office for a psychological screening. I really wanted this to happen. I want to find an adult ally. Someone on my side. Dr. Cooper already knows that I have just been let out of jail. I am going to let it out that I had an abortion. Next, I'm going to hash it out with him.

"Your girlfriend has told you that she has had an abortion?" the doctor asks.

"Yes. I went with her to a clinic."

"So now you are here. Your life is in shambles. How are you getting along?"

"I have been on a couple of different emotional modes, but I don't see my goals change. I'm still on my way to college."

"You are a caretaker. How are you coping with your parents?" The doctor asks.

I tell him, "Whatever life has thrown at me I shoulder. I constantly shoulder it, I guess."

"So is this like a weight you are carrying around. I hear you telling me that you don't think it's fair."

I think of the American soldiers Mr. Soth described in class. They were a rough-and-tumble group. Loyal friends. Fighting machines. Up for an adventure. That's me. That is how I feel. "No. That's not what I'm saying," I answer.

I hear, "Hmm."

My plan doesn't seem to be working either: (a) because this doctor has his own agenda, or (b) he just doesn't understand there are people that won't let this go. I am left to fight on my own. I am having a difficult time communicating with the doctor. Even the exchange at the end of the session was weird. I didn't know if I should shake his hand. I start to raise my hand, but decide a second later not to make the offer. I see his arm jerk.

"I am going to fix your wagon," Mom says as we drive to the social security office. I'm pretty sure she can get it done. I have a two o'clock appointment. My dad runs through my mind. So does Heidi. I am not oriented. I really feel like I have been caught off guard. I'm not prepared for what's next.

Mom and I have sat down on the only two chairs at Betty Yara's desk. Like the other fifty employees, she has a cubicle office. After "hello," her head goes down and her hand moves. I have never met with this lady, but she is writing my name on a manila folder. It is filled with pages of paper. It's at least an inch thick. When I ask her about the file, she tells me, "I have a report from the psychiatrist who screened you."

Dr. Cooper doesn't think I have it together. He told me that he understood the abortion to be a parapraxia. I had to look up the big word he used. It's a Freudian slip. Some kind of blunder. Like I'm a goof. The most serious take away was this:

He did not believe that I could be a consenting adult. He says, "You have to ask yourself if the choices you make will be acceptable later? You had sex. Then you had an abortion. They were completely not acceptable only later in the same week. I think that you only regret your action."

Great. Just superb shit.

His report has sunk me.

Betty Yara starts the interview. She is just taking these pages off of a pile. Going from top to bottom. She asks for not much more than my name and social security number. Twenty minutes later, she is done. She stands and says, "Thank you. The Giving Office will contact you."

It hasn't been much of a fight. Her business was so smooth she couldn't be opposed. My file is now two inches thick. I walk out with my tail between my legs. Only weeks later, I am enrolled in social security disability. Government assistance pay. I read an article on welfare reform that said the surplus in social security will some day be gone. Do these people know where their money is going? Collecting a social security check is important mostly to an older person.

Mom cannot get along without a cane these days. She has gradually become the Riddle of the Sphinx. Someone on three legs. She's all wise. "Now we'll both get our degrees," she says. And I remember that I am now a fully enrolled student at the school of hard knocks.

"As said is done," I say.

I have been navigating through my life. I spent a night in jail. I am a bird that has just flew the cage. The psychiatrist sent me to the psych ward for a night. It was a nightmare vacation. It isn't always so easy. There is a lot to learn.

I've been swallowed whole.

Presently, it seems that Mom only sees an abortion when she looks at me. She has started to antagonize me. Last weekend I was doing yard work. I was sculpting the bushes. I had been outside most of the morning. When Mom came out, she saw the pile of overgrowth I had cut off. She stopped her car in the driveway. She yelled out through her open window, "You are going to kill the bushes."

Mom gets angry, but I don't let it change my mood. I stay steady. Very levelheaded. I ride it out. If I am in the right place at the right time, maybe I can climb out of this hole. I've learned how I can be more of a help. I do all of the easy tasks. I want Mom to come to know me better.

Without being asked I vacuum, pick up groceries, and go with her when she has an appointment to see her doctor.

CHAPTER NINETEEN

Heidi

Bailey Wilson called. I haven't talked to her since the summer. She tells me she has been working at an amusement park. The park puts on events. Bailey is employed as a performer. This weekend is their last show for the season. They are closing things out with a meet and greet. She asks me to come visit.

I was going to a new high school my junior year and kept a low profile. When school started the next fall, I saw a flyer asking people to audition for the school play. I had not made any friends at Lincoln. I wanted some exposure. It was my senior year. I thought the play would be a good way to improve my social life. I got a part. I met Bailey while we were doing the play. She was the stage manager. Everyone knew Bailey was the girl in charge of the theater. She could answer all of the questions asked.

Bailey didn't have time to leave the theater. We made a deal. I got Bailey hooked on Boiled Bunny energy drinks. So I would make a daily run to pick up two. It was my first time in a play. Bailey showed me around the theater. She became my first real friend at the school. Later, we were doing rehearsals for the spring musical. I played the lead role. We were like two peas in a pod.

When the year ended, Bailey invited everyone involved with the theater to her house. The whole cast came. Mr. Stace also came. He is the student advisor and the theater's director and practically lives in the media center. Bailey cried through the entire party. She got really drippy. We had to bring her a box of tissues. "This is my senior year," she sniffled. "I just don't want theater to end."

From the city it's about an hour drive to the park. I listen to my *Alpha Cash* audiobook. I get to the park and leave my car in the lot. I go to guest services. At the window, I buy a ticket. After I show them my ID, they give me a backstage pass.

The park has an outdoor theater. It's a windy day. I want to hear the actors over the noise of the gusts. I look for a seat close to a speaker. I'm in my seat fifteen minutes early. I am trying to read through the program I picked up, but the pages are flapping in the wind. The program reads that the show is about four rowdy travelers who get off a train and get into a saloon. The men in the show become a nuisance. They drink whiskey and cheat at cards. They carouse with the women. The proprietor of the bar chases them out, and they leave town.

It's an all-ages show.

When the show is over, I go backstage. I get about as close as ten feet away from Bailey before I am backpedaling. She is in the center of a circle swelling around her. The cast is doing some team building. Bailey is straight off the stage. I can hear her enunciating every word like her performance hasn't ended. I immediately remember the last conversation I had with her. We had graduated from Lincoln and were talking about our plans. She and I wanted to go straight into our careers.

I decide to let them finish.

There are fifteen makeup tables in the room. Her name is written on the tape stuck to the back of a chair. I take a seat. On the desk in front of me, there is a pile of photos. They are 8 x 11 sized. The first few that I look through are just headshots. Shortly, I get to a picture of the cast of our high school musical. There is a note from Mr. Stace. It says, "Break a leg at the park." I peel off the sticky note paper and look at the photo. We took the picture at the first *Weekdays* dress rehearsal. I was seated in the front row. Everyone else was standing behind my chair.

I don't see myself. I start at the back row and look at each face. No. I'm not in the picture. This photo has been edited. Everyone is leaning toward the center, but I am airbrushed over. In my place, someone has put a potted plant. I know what this is about. A minute later someone vocalizes what I'm thinking. The girl sitting at the table next to me is on her cell phone. She is in the middle of a sentence, before raising her voice to say, "Abortion."

From across the room, another girl follows, "Whore."

I scan the room. I see Ron walking to me. He goes to college in the city and must be here to see Bailey. There is someone dressed as a squirrel with him. When they get to my chair, the squirrel does this lewd dance. Ron shrugs.

I don't think they know each other. The squirrel is rubbing his body on my leg. He is trying to take my hand. Then the lead of the show comes over. I read in the program that his name is Everette. He says to the squirrel, "Go brush your tooth."

When they leave, it's Ron and me. He says, "Nice to see you." Ron and I talk about the city for a few minutes. He has put on a lot of weight since the summer. He tells me he doesn't like college but that his twin sister, Rae, really does.

The team breaks and Bailey comes over. She is still in her stage makeup. She plays a woman in charge of the brothel. She gives me a hug.

"I'm not perfect," I say.

"It's a souvenir. It makes you one of a kind."

Ron says, "It's a derring-do."

"Who told?" I ask.

"Dominic is my boss. He had to get names for the meet and greet. He was writing your name down on the invited list. He was talking about you. Nasty gossip. Everyone in line heard."

Our high school has a very strong theater program. It's well known in the state. Dominic was trained at the Lincoln program. At the time, Bailey and I were only in middle school. Every year there are kids from Lincoln that graduate and study theater in college or are hired in the city as actors. Graduates stay connected to the Lincoln theater. Many alumni give to the program. Unfortunately, the boosters' money shouts no at this alum.

"I really wanted this job. Dominic is the guy who put in the word to get me hired. He can be harsh, but I have bills to pay," Bailey admits.

Everette's at the makeup table next to us. He has taken off the oversized cowboy hat. He has laid it on the counter in front of him. I can see more of him. He's a hottie. While looking at us in his mirror, he says, "I get it. Dominic has outed you."

Now I'm treading water.

Bailey takes us to a huge tent. Ron and I have our guest passes hanging around our necks. We get in smoothly. Ron goes to get us some food. Bailey says, "I hung around with the twins all summer. I'm sure Rae could see me flirting with Ron."

"Have you two been dating?"

"We've only been talking by phone. He's always with his twin. I'm not sure Haley broke up with him because he was a senior. It probably had more to do with his sister." She laughs. "I think the glue holding their bond together has expired."

"This is the first time you two have been alone?"

"Yeah. I had invited them both to the park. Rae wouldn't leave her school's campus, but Ron is staying all weekend."

When Ron comes back, he is with Everette. Bailey introduces him to me. She calls him "Eve."

He asks me some questions. "Do you think I have stage presence?"

He has changed out of his costume and is in his street clothes. I definitely like his looks, but it's too early, so I say, "You are out of your costume." I bite at my food. It's a corn on a stick. "Which one are you?" I act completely puzzled.

He is taken aback. "Yes. Wait. What?" He is about to challenge my bluff. He brings his index finger to his lips and then points it at me. "You're on," he says. "Yes, I wear a white hat. I play the owner of the saloon."

We are all making some small talk, until I see Bailey's smile drop. "Dominic is here. Let's duck and run," she says.

Eve leaves with us and says, "I have a card from Silverbank. We can get a room at the motor lodge." When we get to the Oasis, I go with him to see the manager. He gets two rooms. He put them both on his credit card. "We can work out the roommates later," he says. Eve already has come to my rescue. Still, I am not sure what to make of this guy. My metabolism slows at his suggestion. I drop my arms and lean to the side. The lodge has cookies and coffee twenty-four hours a day. I have some.

In the room, Bailey, Ron, and Eve are having a conversation. I listen.

"I wanted to get my proverbial foot in the door," says Bailey about her job as a performer. I'm sure being a director is more likely her goal.

"I finished high school three years ago and got a job at the park. There is a good career path for a grad in the hospitality industry." I do the math. Eve is twenty-one.

"I'm no longer in high school either," Ron says. "I have school loans, but I couldn't ask my parents to pay my way. I wouldn't have any credibility."

Bailey and Ron start to couple. They are sitting on the bed. They have their backs on the headboard, legs crossed, and shoes off. Eve and I are sitting next to each other on chairs.

"I had this made for you." Eve gives me a charm. There is a picture of his character on one side, and some words on the other. It says: "To: Heidi, From: Eve." They have an arcade here. He made it on a mechanical press. All you do is pick the letters and punch them onto a metal coin. He's such a bling-bling. I am wearing a choker around my neck. I take it off to put the charm on. It falls out of my hand. I bend over to pick up the necklace. He can see down the gap in the waist of my pants. I'm wearing yellow bikini underwear.

Bailey is going through a duffle bag. Without looking up, she says, "Showmanship."

We have been talking for hours. Eve and I are getting along well. Dominic may have thrown me into the deep end, but I don't think I will be drowned. At one in the morning Eve says to Ron, "You two can stay here. We'll take the other room."

I look at Bailey. She says nothing. I know she wants us to leave. She wants to be alone with Ron. I'm hooked up with Eve. He's tall and has nice shoulders. His natural blonde curls are shaved down. He wants the same thing everyone wants: love and money. I haven't been with anyone since Liam. I am hesitant, but this isn't such a bad match for me. I have been preparing myself for this moment. I was waiting for it to come back around. I knew I would just get back into the saddle.

When going to our room, Eve sees someone he knows. "This place is crawling with people from the park," he says.

The next morning, I wake while Eve is getting dressed. He tells me, "I'm going to get us breakfast."

Under the sheets I am naked. "Let me use the bathroom and I'll come with you."

I get out of the shower. I wrap a towel around my body and walk out into the room. Eve isn't even here. I get dressed. When Eve returns, he has something for me to eat. Breakfast is a lemon cream cheese danish and a cup of coffee. "I've got to let Bailey know where we are. Do you want to come with me?"

"I'll meet you," Eve declines.

I get to the room. Ron is in the shower. Bailey has a perma-smile. She says, "I have been sending signals for months. We did it last night."

We make eye contact and I ask, "Are you serious?"

The smile hasn't left her face. I can see it sink in deep as she says, "I like Ron Nelson."

We were drinking last night, and I think all of our inhibitions were down. "I slept with Eve," I tell her. I've talked with Bailey about sex before. She just cashed in her virginity. She always says she doesn't think being a virgin at eighteen is that special. Sometimes I think Bailey puts on an act for everyone. Bailey tells me Ron was also a virgin. In fact, she is ecstatic about Ron's virginity. She is probably right about his high school relationship. It was mostly with his twin.

There is a knock at the door, and the shower is turned off. I haven't been in the room five minutes. When I open the door, I see Eve. I say, "I would have waited for you. What were you doing?"

"Nothing. No. It's nothing."

Ron calls from the bathroom. "Would you bring my clothes to the door?" Bailey collects his stuff and heads to the back of the room.

"Let's just go back to our room," I say. I'm sure Ron could use the privacy.

"I have to see Ron. You go ahead."

This is the third time Eve has tried to leave me this morning. He is brushing me off. It makes me think I just had a one-night stand. He must think I'm so stupid. "Do you not want us to be seen together?" I seethe.

"I should have told you where I stand," he whispers.

"Why don't you?" He already told me that he doesn't have a girlfriend. It leaves the abortion. He probably thinks they're stupid too. I brace myself.

"I know that everything is kind of young. Still I would like to be more than friends."

CHAPTER TWENTY

Liam

I hear Mom on the phone. "Come home. I'm not feeling well." She is talking to my sister. Allison lives on her college campus. Mom has been in and out of hospitals for the last four years. Allison thinks it's a false alarm and doesn't want to drive home.

Mom then says, "I'm killing myself."

This is news to me.

Mom is in hospice. A bed has been set up in the den on the first floor. Running along the wall next to her are three bookshelves. Mom has put some pictures and knick-knacks on the shelves. They make up her memories. I see her occasionally look them over. About six nurses are hired to work on a twenty-four-hour rotation. We are all working to give her "the best quality of life possible." They are giving Mom end-of-life care. These are her last few days.

A few visitors come and go. All of them family.

I just got home from school. My cousin Matt stops me as I walk in the door. "That's assisted suicide." He is talking about my mom. He shakes his head, smiles, and says, "No way. No day." Matt's parents have had a divorce. His sole reaction is to be the moral victor in every situation. We are in the kitchen talking. My grandfather and uncle come out of the den. Grandpa Dean has been in with Mom having her sign a will. He has a crew with him. He is even with a notary public.

Things take a turn. I have suddenly lost both parents. There is a funeral to be planned. My mom had been sick for a long time. I knew this day would come. This is nothing like the day of my dad's funeral. I was young. When I look back, I know that I have been through this before. I am more prepared. So I am not that emotional. The hard part was that sense of urgency between Mom and me. We tried to come to terms with each other after the abortion. Eventually she said I was cool as a cucumber. She also said I learned and would always have the capacity to care for others.

I've known my parents for seventeen years. I know where they lived. I've been inside their home. I've seen them dance at a wedding. I remember dad's just laundered lab coats hanging on a bar to dry. Four in a row. He was a researcher. I could give someone a complete summary of their lives. I saw everything. At some point, we all have to face death. So, this is really important knowledge to have. I'm able to walk away from the cemetery feeling crisp.

After the service, lunch trays are set out. We all eat. I have a plate in front of me, but I am just playing with my food. I'm using my fork to turn fruit chunks into mush.

"Hey, Liam." I look up and see my cousin Matt with a shit-eating grin on his face. "Way to go with the ladies."

This is obviously a sore subject. My body gets hot, and my ears turn red. "Big deal."

"Good timing." He knows my parents would weigh in, but they're not here. He holds a hand up to cover the smile on his face.

Matt has heard about the abortion. The word is out. I am a senior in high school talking to someone only

139

fourteen, but it seems like we are on equal footing. If he throws caution to the wind, things will get serious pretty fast. "Right," I say.

"Or bad. Really sorry to hear about your mom. She did really well at making me feel interesting. She always asked me a lot of questions about school."

He has yielded, so I say, "Yeah."

His phone rings. When he moves away to answer, we break eye contact.

From the other room, my uncle Dan is walking his empty plate into the kitchen. When he sees me he stops and shakes his head. He says in a sing-songy voice, "You are going to get a reputation."

The wrinkles in my life are multiplying like the ones on my dress shirt. My chemistry teacher told me to smarten up last week. I had a fast-food employee flip out before I could make an order. She said, "Do you know what you are? You're a male whore."

I told her to have a nice day. I left before she could challenge me more.

From the kitchen, I hear my grandpa say out loud, "It's a towering minute."

I know he is talking to me. He has put things into perspective.

My cousin ends his call. We go outside and around the corner to vape. "It's my friend's older sister's." Matt pulls a mod from his backpack. "It's her old one. She lets him use it, but I'm holding on to it right now." Matt lives about twenty minutes away by car. Next year he starts high school. He will be living in the same county, but in a different city. I wouldn't know this girl.

He hands the mod to me. I try for a lung hit. All I do is cough.

"I've only been vaping since school started. That's when I got this mod. I love the stuff though." Matt takes a hit, puts three fingers to his mouth, and shoots out dozens of tiny smoke rings.

"Can you give me some pointers, please?" I ask.

"If you want people to smoke with, you have to stop coughing."

Matt takes a hit, exhales a smoke ring, and scoots it toward me with his hand. It expands and falls apart before it makes contact. "The thing about my new mom is she had a divorce. It's definitely no, right? I mean she didn't even come to lunch today."

I try another hit, but it tastes like the high voltage of a battery. I cough. Again.

"My new mom is at a deposition. What a bunch of ironic bullshit."

Her being here would have been kind, but Allison and I don't really know her. "Maybe on some other day," I tell him before passing the mod.

Matt takes it back. He uses his hand to push a couple more smoke rings my way. We hear Uncle Dan call, "Matt?"

He offers me the mod. I wave it off. Matt takes one last hit and blows out a cloud. It's fluffy as hell.

We return. Uncle Dan is talking to my grandfather in the garage. After they see us coming, they split up. Uncle Dan and Matt go home. It's just my grandfather and me. He says, "Don't worry about money. You will be getting an allowance."

CHAPTER TWENTY-ONE

Heidi

While I am at Übertrends, Li asks if I can give her a ride home. She is sixteen and still in high school. She is a co-worker, but she only works part time. **I have my pride** when I'm around her. Their family lives on the west side of the city. Li does not have her driver's license. She didn't pass the driver's course or the written test. Even her cousin, who works at the Secretary of State, couldn't help her out. Li doesn't take public transportation. She never has because her mom drives her around. She takes her to school in the morning, picks her up in the afternoon, and drops her off at work. On other days, Li asks a friend for a ride.

Li has family in the Far East. She engages everyone she knows. She says, "My parents were born here. I've been absorbed into this country." She is always spending time with her family. Her parents try to glean her teenage USA sensibilities. They make it a big part of their lives. Whenever I see her mom, she is dressed like Li. Her dad is always texting with her.

"I can give you a ride," I tell her.

It's Saturday and I came in early and am leaving early. I have been boxing up my property. Today is moving day. Tonight, we are going to the club. As soon as the clock says it's two, Li and I are off for the day. I grab my purse from the back. I leave the store with her right behind me.

When we get to the parking garage, I walk down a lane. I am looking in both directions for my car. Fifteen minutes pass, and we have walked the entire section. Twice.

"Have you lost your car?" she asks.

"I parked in section green," I say. I pull out my phone. It's the first thing I bought with my paycheck. "I'm going to call my dad."

Dad tells me that if it was his car, he would have put a lock on the steering wheel. This is advice that I now wish I had earlier. He tells me to call the cops. We hang up, and I dial 911. Li and I walk to the doors that have a Green Level sticker. Thirty minutes later, a cop car pulls up to the door. He doesn't get out of the car. He doesn't even look at us.

I walk up to his window.

"Are you the person that called 911?"

"Yes. My name is Heidi Vessel."

"What can I do for you?"

"I want to report a stolen car."

I can barely hear him over the police scanner, but he asks all of these questions. He wants to know what street I live on. I tell him where I work. Then he asks, "Any customization on the car?"

I think of the bumper stickers I put on the car, and I go into shock. I wonder if that was the key reason my car was stolen. Have I been singled out? The thieves may think I am some kind of mutt. Easy to prey on me. Someone that won't be able to yell out for help and get anyone to care.

When I look at Li, she is still standing by the door. I look back at the cop and say, "Nope. Nothing custom."

Li walks over to us. The dispatcher goes off through the radio. "I've got to take this call," the cop says.

"What else should I do?" The police scanner has been crackling. I think of the registration slip Dad told me to put in the glovebox. The thieves have my home address. I'm practically lost.

"Now, you go to the secretary of state." He puts his squad car into drive, nods his head, and says, "Ladies."

We walk to the ground floor. I follow Li a couple of city blocks. All the way to the secretary of state. Once we are inside, I get into the line. Li goes over to this guy, and they talk. That must be her cousin. She told me that he moved to the big city not too long ago. He is older than me. About thirty. He is wearing a short-sleeved shirt with a collar and a DMV logo. He has on a sporty pair of nylon pants. Li waves at me.

At the desk, the lady gives me a number. Then I find some seating. Li walks away from her cousin. She sits down in the seat I have saved for her. This office is the first thing to close. It closes at five o'clock. The stores in the mall are closed at nine o'clock. I say, "We are going to leave for the club at ten. Do you think your cousin wants to go with us tonight?"

"He is married. They are expecting a baby. He doesn't want to go with us."

My number is called. I go up to the counter. With her computer, the lady starts to process my information. Li's cousin has walked over to the desk. He brings up his hand to wave.

I say, "Hello."

He waves again.

I smile.

He points his finger at me and says, "Tigress!"

I just stare back.

He points again and says, "You are a tigress!"

I realize that this guy is on the job. He is on the lookout for predators. He is making a career out of it, I think. The lady at the terminal dismisses me. I leave the counter touching my face. I look at my arms. I don't feel any orange fur. I don't see any stripes.

I walk up to Li and ask, "You told him?"

"They have abortions in the Far East too. Some couples only want a baby boy. They have them for any reason." She shrugs.

I look once more at Li's cousin. I see that he has made his hand into a claw. He is moving it like he wants to tear something apart. The world can be a dangerous place. I turn around and walk out.

I think I can see suburbia in the rearview mirror.

After leaving the secretary of state, I call Nolan. He is the full-time stock boy at Übertrends. He asks me for the mail every day. We have fallen into a quick exchange with each other. I am starting to learn his game. I know the play here. *Alpha Cash* says that this is a simple transaction.

Earlier in the week, Nolan came up to the front desk for the mail. I said, "I'm standing close enough to you to catch a contact high." I mean, jeez. Smoke much? I remind him of our no smoking store policy and refuse to give him the letters that he wants.

I was kicking butt, until Nolan remembered that I got "vacuumed." He reminded me of the "fetus deletus." At that point, my words lost some meaning. I couldn't live his life for him. We all have choices to make. He won some of my respect. I cheerfully handed over the mail to him.

Today I ask Nolan if he will pick Li and me up from the secretary of state. I invite him to go with us to the club. I tell him that I will pay his way. He takes the offer. Nolan drops Li off at her house. We plan to meet at my place, before we go to the club. He then drives to my parents' house. During the ride, I ask Nolan if he can give me a hand. Nolan will help me move.

In one try, I take all of my stuff from my parents' house. I load everything into Nolan's trunk and onto his seats. His import is packed. On the trip to the apartment, Nolan and I stop by the store. I give him beer money. We pick out some party supplies, like cups and snacks. He's twenty-one and pays at the counter. By eight o'clock we are at the apartment standing in my new room. We are surrounded by piles of my belongings. While I set up the room, we drink and talk.

I get paid minimum wage, and now I am paying rent. I'm living my life paycheck to paycheck. I will have to decorate my room one piece at a time. Not exactly the swishy frills I thought would be surrounding me.

"How do you like working for Cole?" I ask.

"I see him scrape by every day. He lets me do what I want."

"It seems like that job is Sharon's whole life."

"Sharon is hopeless."

This needs an explanation. "What?" I ask.

"Every February she tries to hook Cole on Valentine's Day. Every spring she tries to throw herself onto him. I've never seen her talk to other guys. It seems like the only person she wants to date is Cole, but he always looks past her."

Nolan started working at Übertrends a couple of years before me. He almost never leaves the back room. While away from the customers, I'm sure Cole and Sharon can act naturally. When you get the private show, it is easy to pick up the inside details.

"I didn't know there was something between them."

"Let's just say I have a job."

This guy knows my secret, and I have to work with him. "What? Do you just lose yourself in the soap opera of other people's lives?"

"I like to keep my biz on the hush-hush. So I keep my eyes peeled and my ears opened. When I get the relevant information on somebody, I can use it as a bargaining chip."

I think that this is Nolan's way of getting people to buzz-off.

"Thank you so much for helping me move." Today I play the damsel in distress and say, "So glad you could look past everything and see me."

I invite Li and Tina from the kiosk over to my new place. It's a short distance from the apartment to the club. By ten o'clock, we are all in my kitchen. After we get smashed, we head out to dance.

CHAPTER TWENTY-TWO

Liam

It's Saturday morning. The kitchen is out of food. Like clockwork I am at the grocery store. I pick a cart. When I hear a man yell, "Abortion," I am not ten feet into the store. I turn around to look. There is a guy pointing at me. He wears glasses. He has black hair around the sides of his head but is bald on top. A rim baldy. He turns and exits.

I start walking with my eyes straight ahead. I don't make eye contact with anyone. I push my cart into the frozen foods section. I am looking into the doors. In the reflection, I see a few people come up behind me. When I turn around, I feel pinned to the glass.

A middle-aged hipster with a beard is so close I can feel his hot breath. He says, "Wrongo, dongo."

"Killer," says a woman. She sizes me up with her thumb.

A guy taps the wallet in his back pocket. He calls me "Mr. Moolah" and says, "You think you can't be stopped."

From the next aisle we hear from a man that cannot be seen. "You know him, but I want to remind you he is not alone." It's a strange and mysterious voice.

The stranger is right. These people know me. I have parked all of their cars. These guys know my parents have left me some money. They seem to think I will get away with something. Like I have already been bailed out. The man who has spoken up has put everyone on level ground. I try to wear a brave face with a toothy grin. It doesn't come to me. All I can do are some shaky legs and a faint smile.

"Outlaw," another man cries out. "I can't wait to tell all my friends at the courthouse."

I say, "It's not a crime," but I am practically whispering to myself.

A few bystanders have been attracted to the scene. It's a standoff, but there are no more words. Then everyone abruptly moves on. My awareness is heightened. It's taken to a new level. It feels like I have a sponge inside me, and not a stomach. I look at the deli counter. Nothing looks very good. I walk away. I've always eaten my greens, but I never thought I would become a vegan. I think it may be a thing I should start today. Maybe I will only eat veggies.

I go down a few more aisles. No one is paying any attention to me. I am alone now, but I am also at an impasse. I'm not hungry for anything. A rule has to be made. Don't pick anything that will make you look like a fussy eater. I throw regular Oat O's, packaged chicken breast, hot sauce, and rice into my cart. My diet looks the same as the next guy's. Everything is the same. Something is just a little different, since I just had an abortion. I start to sweat, before I get cold. I speed to the front of the store.

While in line for the checkout my cell phone rings. It's my grandfather.

"Hi, Grandpa."

"Liam, do you have time to get lunch?"

"Yes."

"Great."

When I get home, I park in the garage. I grab the groceries. Once I am inside, I set them on the counter. Allison is home. She and Uncle Dan have been walking through the house. They are trying to collect all of the medical equipment my dad and mom used. Dan already promised a charity they could have the wheelchair. Really, they can have everything. I would like if it could help someone. Grandpa explained that it is sound financially to use a charity. He said, "It's a good tax deduction."

Uncle Dan comes into the kitchen and asks, "Where does your mom keep her spare pair of eyeglasses?" I open a cabinet door to show him where they are kept. She had a few pairs. Those are also going to a charity. Allison comes in with the Grabber. When you squeeze a trigger, two pieces clamp together at the other end. It can pick up anything under five pounds. She gives it to Uncle Dan.

Uncle Dan, Allison, and I are still in the kitchen. The phone begins to ring. My sister answers, and passes the phone over to me. She says, "It's for you. It's Ted Tater from the brokerage house."

Allison looks into the bags. She pulls out the frozen waffles.

After I hang up, they are looking at me. Uncle Dan asks, "What did he say?"

"He is holding money Dad left for me," I answer right before the toaster pops.

On Monday morning, I go to the law office for a meeting. I take a day off from school. A lot of business needs to be done before Allison leaves. We make a plan. We are all going to Ted's office to withdraw money from an account my dad made. Ted has divided the funds and prepared two checks. One for my sister. One for me.

"I know you have some expenses. You will need some money," Grandpa says.

A few things have changed since my father left me this money. That being: (a) my mom has died and, (b) I have had an abortion. At the brokerage house, Uncle Dan says a few things to me. "You are only seventeen. Your mom wanted us to handle your money."

Grandpa Dean tells me, "I want to set up a trust fund."

I am holding the check in my hand. "Give your check to Grandpa," say Allison and Uncle Dan. I look at my grandpa. He makes a sweeping "send it over to me" motion with his hands. After the canvassing I got at the grocery store, I am feeling soft. I better play it cool. So I sign the check and pass it to him.

CHAPTER TWENTY-THREE

Grandpa Dean

We go on a Saturday afternoon to get a sandwich and do some shoptalk. It's Dan, Liam, and me. This is Allison's senior year. She is back on campus. We are talking about what it will take to get his house sold. We agree it needs paint and new carpeting. Dan will be working on who to hire. So that's done. That takes us halfway through lunch. Next we have come to some legal business. That is what I would like to get to while we are all together.

Liam knows I am going to create a trust fund for him. He is only seventeen. To protect him the court will assign a person they call an *ad litem*. I say, "I expect an officer of the court to contact you."

Liam asks, "Why? My parents have already made plans. You said they have provided for me."

I tell Liam, "You are not out of the woods yet."

Dan raises his voice to announce the abortion publicly. Heads turn from the other booths. Liam puts a hand up and drops his head. He has hidden half of his face and is shaking his head. A couple starts talking over their meal. Liam looks through his fingers.

The man says, "Right in our city, too. Remember the neighbor's kids?"

The woman answers, "Icky. I heard they had an abortion."

Our court date is already on the county judge's docket. Judge Cannow allows the public chatter. The Centerville city council members are also talking. They have engaged their voters. The whole town is talking. The conversation is non-stop. There is a mom and dad challenging the current abortion laws. I saw a television interview that our state representative gave. He said, "I have the family in mind, and, as we speak, there is legislation in the works."

Liam asks, "Who are these people? I don't have anything to say to them."

Dan tells him, "What these people say counts. You've got to swallow your pride."

Dan is right. The public can sway our congressmen's vote either way. We are sitting in a booth. I look over the table and lower my voice when I say, "It's all of our futures that I am thinking about."

We are going to the court to set up this trust. It is a sensitive process. The court has already learned that Liam has had an abortion. This will be a tricky case. There is currently open legislation on the procedure in this state. I'll do what I can to remedy Liam's situation as we make our way through the probate court dates.

CHAPTER TWENTY-FOUR

Liam

A guardian ad litem has been assigned to me, since we are going to the probate court. He is acting as a counselor. I have not been making it to class this year. My chemistry teacher noticed. He pulled me aside, and warned me not to miss his class again this semester. It worked out that I could make an afternoon appointment with the ad litem. After school ends for the day, I drive to his office. It's three fifteen and we have a meeting scheduled. He does not have a secretary. I'm left standing in the middle of the front room. When he comes out of his office, I immediately recognize him.

It's rim baldy. My jaw drops.

"You were at the grocery store the other day," I state.

"Yeah. We go to the same store."

His office is across the street from the store I shop at for groceries. I say, "You were the guy yelling and pointing at me."

"So?"

He arrogantly waves at me to follow him into his office, but I shake my head, and , say, "No." I stand there stunned. He then comes up to me. We are both standing. He says, "Yes," and calmly starts talking. He explains the purpose and procedures of the court. "Your parents have left you their money. Your grandfather wants to open a trust fund at the court. He is asking to be named as the trustee. Do you object?"

All of the money is to go toward things I need. The trustee holds and hands out the cash. I love my grandfather. I am learning a ton. He can be trustee. There is a different problem I am having. It's with this man. "You told a group of strangers about the abortion." I go on to tell the ad litem that I did not ask to become a public figure.

"There is a big stink being made," the ad litem says.

"I am worse off after becoming an open book to the public." People hear about the abortion and are quick with their nos.

Grandpa and Uncle Dan know that I have a yes policy on the procedure. The ad litem tells me that I am a protected person. I think about the suicide girl. As the mom and dad fight Congress for new abortion laws, they are actively involved with the public debate. People always put it out there when I am around. The topic comes up at the supermarket, restaurants, and just about everywhere I go.

I am just twisting in the wind.

The ad litem goes on to some old business. "Your parents paid into the system but died before they could collect. You have been collecting a disability check. The court will try to be fair. You could continue collecting social security checks."

I would not like to continue on the government assistance program. I get labeled as disabled. Everyone involved with me is gagged. The people I know won't be able to vouch for me. They can't fight the Social Security Administration. They would get crushed under the weight. Besides, people have their own obstacles. I just couldn't ask them to smooth the bumps on my road.

Beyond the social security checks, I now have an inheritance.

I don't want the public assistance. I say, "No thanks."

He says, "Fine, Liam. We also need to talk more about the abortion. When we go to court you will be standing in front of a decision-maker. He will decide if you and Heidi made a clean break." Again, I think of the mom and dad whose teenage daughter had an abortion. They have gotten media attention. Their complaint will send our state representatives into a vote about the procedure. Rim baldy says, "It's not likely that the trust fund will be finished and working any time soon." He explains about the catch in my case. He says, "You will be eighteen. You may have a trust. Still that will be pushed into the background. The prospect of new abortion legislation is now in the front of people's minds."

I ask, "I'm just a picayune case, aren't I?"

The ad litem says, "Maybe, but I do think this is something that is going to hold the judge's attention."

This is one for the ages.

After leaving the ad litem's office, I stop by Udders to eat. I must have some sugar. The cow is in clothes today.

He is wearing a suit with a vest. I find an open table and sit. It's a cold and rainy day outside. I should have brought him a cup of Flannel Dutch tea. A few people come into the eating area, but drop their voices when they see me. No one sits close to me. I can see them look at me peripherally, though. A couple of students look at me with worry.

When I get home, I look at my reflection in the mirror. I have a rash. I started the third button on my shirt in the wrong hole. A clump of my hair sticks out.

The next afternoon, I go to the CPC cemetery. There are acres of land here. It is huge. It takes some searching before I find my parents. I see their markers. They are side by side. "I see Grandpa Dean and Uncle Dan," I say. "They tell me I can call them for any reason." Grandpa and Uncle Dan seem to think I need to be looked after. I am talking to the markers. I tell them, "They ask if there is anything I need, but I never have anything in mind." I didn't even know where to start. Talking has been a good place, I guess. Nothing will work if we don't communicate with each other. The words are slowly coming. I'm not sure what else I have to say. I blank and decide to leave.

CHAPTER TWENTY-FIVE

Heidi

It's true that when Liam came to the city, it was like we were a very together couple. We were at home alone. We ate all of our meals together. We cuddled. We woke up in the same bed. Then, we schemed about the kind of business we would pull at the clinic.

High on my *Alpha Cash* list of what's important are my people. I haven't talked to Liam since that day at the clinic. I feel like I left him with a frown. I don't want him to feel rejected. I don't think we will ever forget each other. I have an impulse that is surging. I want to call him. I want to text him. I want to friend him on my social media pages. In the end, I don't believe that we did much more than sleep together.

I've decided to see Eve again. We've been texting back and forth and talking by phone. I have put pictures of him onto my PicturePost site. I seem to make him happy. Eve calls to say he will pick me up at four. We are going to my parents'. It was actually them that reached out to me. It has been a while since I had any face time with them. I will let them in on a part of my life. I will introduce them to my boyfriend. According to *Alpha Cash*, sharing Eve is like giving my parents fifty bucks.

When we get onto my parents' porch Eve says earnestly, "I think my sex life should be kept private."

"I don't think they will ask," I say. I knock on the door. It wasn't too long ago that I was moving out of this house. I surrendered my set of house keys. I left them on the kitchen table and then I dragged out my last load.

"You said they had a hand in everything 'Heidi.'"

This isn't like the time I got a prescription for the pill and Mom said, "I want you to remember, Heidi, that boys like you. A lot. Make him wait for his lucky day."

I am eighteen and have moved out of my parents' house. I don't ask them for money, because I have a job.

I am on my own to make my own choices. "I have a job. They have less sway now," I say before the door opens.

We all sit down. Eve is telling us his story. When he was a teen, he worked very hard. He worked at a state park. He would repair and keep the bicycle rentals on the trails. By his senior year, he had saved enough money to buy his own car. He picked a shiny red mustang. Eve is winning us all over. Work is something we have in common. We are both driven. I tell him I am impressed.

My phone rings. I go into the next room to talk. I can hear the buzz of a conversation continue for the few minutes the call I take lasts. When I return everyone stands. Eve and I leave. On the way out, Dad pats me on the back. I had to stop by his house. Even after the abortion. I want him to see that I haven't just dropped out of his life.

From my parents' house we go to a restaurant. Eve takes me to this Spanish place called Garcia's. He wants to order a dish called paella for me. Eve says, "You'll love it. It's the best." While we are at dinner, I suck my drink out of a straw. My cheeks suck in like a fish face. Eve looks at me amused and makes a funny face. When the waitress returns I tell her, "I ordered diet. This is regular."

Our food comes a few minutes later. They have served us the wrong order. We do not know the people working at this restaurant. I don't have the relevant information on them. Yet the abortion comes up. People at the other table watch. However, there is no exchange of information and we cannot bargain. We are losing. Finally, someone verbalizes that the waitress is gay. She is now on her heels. Eve tells her, "I work just as hard as you." He takes out his wallet and puts some money on the table. Then we just leave. Eve explains that he has zero tolerance for people that won't show us respect.

Eve is hungry when we get to the apartment. I have everything I need to make margaritas. I crush ice and put salt around the rim of the glasses. I am going to pair our drinks with the burritos that are in the freezer. I put them into the oven. It is going to be intimate with just the two of us. Everything. The kitchen floor is wet as I put out dishes. I slip and fall. I injure myself and call out to Eve. He swoops in and carries me out to the car. Then he runs back inside to turn off the oven.

The hospital won't just give me a wrap and send me home. The ER doctor treating me is determined to find the cause of all of these crashes I have had. He doesn't know the particulars, but asks, "Has this happened before?" I am afraid to say yes, but I do. The staff scan me, prick me, X-ray me, and take my fluids. By 2:00 a.m., the doctor has ruled out a dozen notions. He tells me to make an appointment with an optometrist.

For the moment my twisted ankle needs some ice and my wrist is in a splint. My health insurance will put some money in for the bill. I count my blessings.

After four short hours of sleep, I wake up to Eve laughing. I go into the bathroom. My roommates were with their boyfriends last night. They haven't returned. I figure Eve is on the phone. I am washing my face and listening. All I can make out from here is something about a job opportunity. After showering I am back in my room. I hear more laughing.

I put on a jumper, but leave most of it unbuttoned.

Eve is on the phone. He has a notepad and pen in front of him. He has jotted down a bunch of notes. There is more laughing before he gets off of the phone. From the kitchen table he looks up at me and says, "I'll have juice first. I also want egg whites and toast. Three eggs."

I pour two glasses of juice and tell him, "I don't have any eggs."

Eve says, "I like egg whites. They are a good source of protein for me."

I glare at him and raise my arm to point to the splint.

"Yeah," he chuckles. "I was happy to be here to help you out."

"What time did you wake up?" I ask.

"I've been up for over an hour or two. I was waiting for you."

"My roomies will be back, and I will see what I can do about the supermarket," I acquiesce.

He says, "I have some business today."

"When we were at my parents', I got a call to be in for a shift at work," I tell him. One of the girls that works part time asked me to cover for her. Some guy she just met wants to take her to a hockey game. She told me, "I really, really want to go."

This is why we haven't been able to get together too often. We are both always working. Work is a high priority for me. I want a career. Eve has already showered and is dressed. It's late fall. There is a chill in the air. He takes his jacket off the back of the chair. I am standing in the middle of the kitchen as he comes up to kiss me. My eyes follow him. He goes to the oven and opens the door. The burritos from last night are still lying on the baking sheet. "Don't forget to clean this," he says before he leaves.

I'm nonplussed.

CHAPTER TWENTY-SIX

Mom Vessel

Our house in the city has a small backyard. There is a mature oak tree practically in the center of the lawn. The calendar says it's November, and the tree has lost all of its leaves. It's the weekend. My husband and I are outside doing yardwork. We are both wearing sweatshirts. There is a transfer on them from Lincoln High School Drama.

At first blush, I had a talk with Liam. This was before the move to the city. He was at our house sitting on a lounge chair by the pool. I thought Liam was grappling with the loss of his father. I also had a talk with Heidi. I told her he was doing the best he could.

She told me that his mother was sick. I remembered that Heidi was his first girlfriend. Liam's emotions were already running high. I didn't know what was about to happen. Though Heidi had a precaution. She went on the pill.

We have been working for over an hour. My husband is starting from the edges of the lawn and raking the leaves into the middle. We have been getting dry weather. All of the leaves are rusty reds, browns, and golds. Even if they are brittle, they're easy to work with. I have been putting the leaves into brown paper yardbags, but there is still a tall pile.

I used to think a little bit of competition was healthy. My husband and daughter go at it as I watch. The last few months have been hard. They really challenge each other. When her father was growing up, his teachers always made him out to be slow. They thought he had one tire stuck in the sand. His senior year of high school they wouldn't graduate him. He thought the school system was a bunch of bull, until he got his GED.

He knows Heidi had a procedure. He thinks she has fallen into business.

My thoughts on what she has done about the pregnancy? I've been in medical billing for fifteen years. For all of the women, the procedure should be a real solution. What's tough is people aren't always so agreeable. I see that happen. There is one thing her mother would like her to know:

If you have an abortion, it's at your expense. Sorry.

When my husband has put all of the leaves into the pile, he leans the rake against the house. He walks up to me and grabs a couple of the stuffed bags. He will drag them to the front yard. The garbage truck will take them away.

My husband says, "We don't see Heidi so much these days."

"No. It was nice to see her last night, but it's time to let it go." Heidi will always be our daughter, but she is grown. Heidi's a young adult. There is little more my husband and I can do for her.

After graduating high school, Heidi went right into the job market. She is on pretty solid ground. In a lot of ways, she is following in her dad's footsteps. Heidi will not go to a university. She left school with a plan to get early experience at a job. I think that says a lot about her. She wants a sales position. She doesn't need an advanced degree. She won't be in debt. She will one day be rewarded for her experience. As soon as Heidi settles into a job, it could turn into a long career.

CHAPTER TWENTY-SEVEN

Liam

The Tenth Judicial Circuit Court is where the county judges have chambers. That is where the **great** literature of the law is read. A place where the attorney is made into something strong. The court says that this is just a hearing. It may not be likely, but this whole situation could just end today.

My uncle Dan pulls me aside as I enter the lobby. "You don't like the law game?"

"Everyone just builds their cases. I think they are only helping themselves," I answer.

He asks, "What about the ad litem?"

"Even worse."

Uncle Dan says, "I heard things got pretty rough at the grocery store."

"Yeah," I tell him. "They really did."

"Just a guy trying his luck," he says about rim baldy. "Don't let anyone trip you up."

At the checkpoint into the building is a guard. He collects everything on your person. You then walk through a metal detector. While I am waiting in line, I hear him chit-chat with a couple of people. I see them become fast friends. They definitely broke the mold after they made this guy. While he is waving the detection wand over me he asks, "Are you ready for your day in court, chief?"

The ad litem told me that this case can't be taken lightly. People get into alliance just on their disapproval of abortion alone. They get some funding. They have leaders who will come forward. They will be using their usual arguments. Right now there is a mom and dad case in our state. They are against the procedure and have been very outspoken. There might be new legislation.

"Not looking to break new ground here," I tell him.

Once you are actually in the building it's esoteric. Everything is made of marble. If the walls could talk, I would discover the people that have walked these halls.

There must be eight million stories. Lots and lots of people who have had a lapse in morals have had business here.

I think of my case. There is not an ending in sight. I'm just not sure.

The ad litem is standing outside the courtroom. I walk up to him. "The judge has a file on you," he says. "It's this thick." He holds his hands about a foot apart. A file that big must contain all of the details of my life. The court knows that I have had an abortion. Rim baldy tells me, "The judge may put a holding on you until everything has run through Congress."

A lot of those pages have only a name and street. I hit back. I take a jab at the court. I laugh and say, "I can read that bulk in one day."

We go into the courtroom and find a place to sit on the benches. Grandpa is also here. He is sitting on one of the benches, but on the other side of the courtroom. I think about the fight on abortion brewing outside. I'm sure the judge will take the safest position possible. Once my case is called, the guardian ad litem and I go up to a table.

I stand in front of the judge. He is going through my file. That is a load of paper. So far, the doctor that screened me has mailed in a complete report. My uncle

Dan has written the court a letter saying I can't multi-task. He is still on a kick because what I fed Mom wasn't cholesterol-free. My credit report showed that I had no credit history. I hope the guardian ad litem has been fair with his recommendation. Nonetheless, the brass has put over their business. That's for sure.

"Okay, let's go to the motions," Judge Cannow starts.

Grandpa says, "Liam's parents have died. We are here today to put a trust fund into place."

The court has not dismissed my Grandpa being the trustee. I am seventeen and I'm certain that there will be a trust. My parents have died. Nobody else could make it run. He got the job by default. The guardian ad litem stands and says, "That is not being contested by his grandson."

The mom and dad have been out in front of the public as the people debate abortion procedures. So have I. Uncle Dan thinks people won't want my business during this legislative confusion. For example, none of the brokerage houses want to manage my money. Uncle Dan wrote about this in the letter he gave the court. He says, "The trust fund will dwindle."

Grandpa is painting this picture for the court. It's up to the judge to buy or not. "I would like Liam to have the income from the social security checks. I am going to pay the bills with this money. I will do what I can to conserve the trust fund."

Receiving these checks has been something I would very much like to end. Keeping everything on track the ad litem says, "Liam doesn't want the Social Security Administration to represent him. He will be the beneficiary of a trust."

The judge is wilting under the onus. He makes a judgment. "Well, you have brought this case to me," he says to Grandpa Dean. "After reading the file, I know there is a lot more going on. This case is going through my courtroom. While this is happening, you might as well get the social security checks."

He slaps his gavel, and everyone scatters.

Grandpa is going through the steps the court asks to make the trust operational. During this process the abortion came to light. The judge has read it in my file. We look at each other. The judge isn't going to let me slide. As I collect social security checks I will continue to be a part of the rotation in the public debate. It seems to me that I have just become the poster boy of abortions for this courtroom. It seems to me that I have only begun to learn how to fight.

I would like to take the court bailiff's badge off of his uniform and crumple it in my hand.

I have a follow-up appointment with my academic counselor. Mr. Herald says, "I haven't seen you come to my office. So I called you in myself. I want to know how the college applications are going."

"I haven't filled out any college applications," I say.

Mr. Herald says, "Okay. I'll give you some space."

I tried to reject the Social Security Administration, but Judge Cannow has assigned it to me. It just feels like I have been caught up in the abortion debate. It never was my intention to argue for abortion publicly. I mean, I don't want to do it out loud. I don't want to debate this with strangers. Yet I do every time that I am out. I am challenged by people every day. When I am challenged, I push back. We fight about the abortion.

They say, "You can't have one."

I say, "Yes you can."

The next day we do the whole thing over again.

I tell Mr. Herald about my dilemma. I admit to him that I think a person would really have to be strong to survive out there in the world.

He says, "When your dad died. When your mom died. I've seen you get back up."

"All I can do is go onward," I say.

"Sisyphus was an inmate in Hades," Mr. Herald tells me. "He rolled a boulder up a mountain. When he would come up close to the top, the boulder would roll back to the ground. He must have done it a thousand times. The point I'm trying to make is that it will take as much brains as it takes brawn."

CHAPTER TWENTY-EIGHT

Heidi

I'm surfing the web, and I come across a headline. Xclothing has gotten some negative publicity. That is a clothing brand that Cole features at his store. Our government's Department of Labor has opened an investigation. The article says Xclothing's alleged use of children in the production of its clothing takes place at an overseas factory. It is written the children are working twelve-hour days and are paid low wages.

At the end of the article, I read that any donations will help to fight this illegal business. A not-for-profit has set up a link. I press the button. It takes me to a web page where I fill out a questionnaire. I make a money contribution as well. An e-mail is sent back with a receipt and a response. It reads as follows:

Unlimited Protest's (UP) was started ten years ago by Lance Knupp. After graduating from college, he joined the workforce. Growing up he had heard of questionable business done in American industry. Lance soon found the company he worked for was embroiled in a controversy. He decided to take action. His activism champions human rights causes.

Time to put my plan into action. The abortion cost me big time. I need to find a way to get clients. The ladies at the smokehouse in the mall hand out free samples of jerky to attract customers. I think volunteering is the best possible way to reach people. Get them to know me in a well-rounded way. Really move people to my side. Lance has set up an office in the city to stop Xclothing. I'm going to drop in on them. Maybe I'll be invited to join.

The next day, I check the bus schedule. An hour later, I'm dropped off on the sidewalk looking into UP's office. It's in a strip mall and from the knees up is all windows. There is someone standing at the door. Without stopping I pull the door open and walk inside.

"When young people take action, they can make it happen." A guy has his hand out for a shake. I think of my dad and remember to look him in the eyes. "Hi, I'm Curt," he says. "Just checking on the weather."

I show him the receipt I printed out from my computer. Then I find myself following Curt around the makeshift office. "Heidi," he starts. "This is Kyle. He is our media team. You'll find him writing a blog and setting up links." Kyle was typing on his computer, but he takes a minute to look up. Curt says, "This is Jean-Pierre. He has a team. They do all of the footwork." Beyond him there are stacks of signs on sticks. They are leaning against the wall. "This is Lance. Last but not least." He laughs.

Lance is sitting behind a desk that is completely void. He says, "We all do our share."

He's pretty interesting, I guess. I wondered what kind of a guy would collect donations and organize protests for a living. I didn't know what to expect. I thought he might dress casually and wear wire-rimmed eyeglasses. Like the guy I saw running for our high school class president. He wore that during the debate. That is not how he looks. The first thing I notice is all of the buttons he has stuck to his shirt.

I introduce myself.

Lance says, "I read through your online submission. We are about to make our first move. You are exactly who we need. The media is going to love you. It will be Xclothing's own customer that will be making our demands heard. The CEO can't help but listen to us."

I tell them, "The owner of the store that I work at does business with Xclothing. Cole may be in a bad deal." This is true. It calls for a protest. I am also counting on my work with UP to help jump-start my career. I quickly learned that as an actress I am in the business of selling myself. *Alpha Cash* says as much. I am building my own personal brand awareness. People will see that I care about social issues.

Curt says, "You can get involved right now."

"How?" I ask.

Jean-Pierre comes up with his arm full of signs. "I'm going to put these signs into my car. At twelve o'clock, all of the picketers are going to meet. We will be walking in front of the Xclothing corporate office building."

Lance asks, "Will you go with them?"

"It's a nice day outside," Curt coaxes.

Once all of the signs are in his car, we are off.

At noon everyone grabs a sign. They are professionally done. The signs read No to Child Labor. We walk in a circle. We are in a groove as a television rig drives up to the curb. It's from Channel 5.

A crew gets out of the van. They set up their equipment. We stop walking to watch. The station sent a seasoned anchor to do the report. She is helped out of the van and gets to her mark. It's a black reporter named Gwen Host. I'm standing about twelve feet away. She shuffles through a stack of index cards, before dropping a few. Some are carried by the wind and land at my feet. I pick them up. When I look up, Gwen is staring at me. She has a grin rising on her face. A man hurries over but is halted. Gwen asks me to bring her the cards.

Gwen has been sitting behind the station's desk and reading the news for years. "Sorry," she says. "I'm not in the field often." She looks me up and down. When all of the cards are collected, she puts them in her pocket. She asks, "Do you care if I interview you?"

Jean-Pierre is walking to us with an objecting hand in the air. Someone from the news crew says to him, "We need to see you guys walking with your signs."

"You'll look able," Gwen promises Jean-Pierre. "It will make the eleven o'clock news."

It is only a matter of time before everyone hears that I have had the procedure. I will be scrutinized, but I am not out of place. I know that I look like the hundreds of customers that buy the Xclothing brand. Actually, I have bought the brand before. We may be funding illegal business. The CEO can't do that to us. I have no time left to double-check my math. I cannot back out. This is my best shot at a career. We turn on the mark, and the cameraman records me answering Gwen. The rest of the gang are holding signs and walking in the background.

"Do you own any clothing from Xclothing?" Gwen asks.

"Yes, but I had different expectations. I think they can do better."

On the bus ride home, I think about the day. People will trust me when they see me on TV. I need to reach out to the market. I would like people to walk away from Xclothing. The people who get my message will see that I'm not just in it for the attention and money. The CEO is doing bad business, and I am calling him out. Overall, it's some goodness.

That night I am home at eleven and in my room. I turn on Channel 5 and see the protest. Gwen has made a charged report. I got marked as being a former Xclothing customer. I have some good feelings about the day. Still, I do not know what will happen between Cole and me. I hope today will make him into a "Heidi" fan. The report also had a statement from the Xclothing CEO, who said, "Our business practices are on par. We will take action against anyone that says they are not."

Liam

I answer my phone and hear, "You can see Heidi. I have her on a memory stick."

It's my friend Gavin. "Is this my bro with video?" I ask.

"Hey, Liam. How was your Thanksgiving?"

I don't remind Gavin that it's weird to celebrate the holidays without my mom or dad. "Meh. There are 365 days in a year. I don't have a favorite."

After Bailey saw Heidi on the news, she called Lincoln's media center to give them the scoop. There was a time when Heidi was the darling of Lincoln theater. Mr. Stace put the audiovisual team on the story. They called

Channel 5 to request a copy of the recorded protest. Our school's *Walking and Talking* show will air a segment on their alumnus and activist:

Heidi Vessel.

I pick up my cousin Matt, and we meet Gavin at our school. He is in the media room. Matt knows I was sent to jail. We are having an argument. He says, "You are in the public eye. People are going to think of you as a bruiser."

Having a trust fund keeps people at a distance. Although, it doesn't take long for people to hear that I am also collecting social security assistance. After, the public finds me much more approachable. "You don't know what it takes," I say critically.

"I saw you fight."

I can't be heard over the abortion. It's the only thing people can remember. People walking by me are always calling me out. They are always throwing it back at me. I say, "I think it's better than being a pushover."

"I know, but there are better ways to handle the dicks."

Gavin says, "I can already see the religious missionaries at your door."

I always hear of people that find salvation in religion. "It might as well happen," I say.

Matt asks, "Religion?" Then he answers, "It's real simple. If you can't beat them, join them."

This is practically becoming a religious experience. And I could use a miracle right about now. "I don't root against God," I tell them.

"If you could just see it my way," Gavin says persuasively. "Look at me. I'm a novelty. Do you know what we have in common?"

Gavin's face is framed by his hairline. His bright auburn hair is as thick as carpeting. He wears long sideburns. He is tattooed and has pierced his head three times. Gavin is always in the hallway pushing a cart filled with equipment from the media center. I can't even remember the last time I saw him in Mr. Soth's history class.

"What's that, Gavin?"

"We would be liked by anyone's tastes. We tickle appetites."

Now I know how Gavin manages to sidestep his classes. I swear he's an angel.

Gavin plugs the flash drive into the player and says, "Let's see what we've got here."

At 20:35 Gwen takes some index cards from her pocket. She is holding a microphone and shuffling through the cards. Heidi is waiting for the questions. Many cards separate from the pile, and for the second time that day fall. Heidi and Gwen instinctively bend. They bang heads before the cards can be picked up. Someone from the crew responds. The cards are handed back to Gwen.

The camera is on the whole time and picks up everything. Gavin says, "This is the uncut version. Look at how damn woozy that anchor got. No wonder the eleven o'clock broadcast only included one question. That's all they could get out. I can't believe it, but Gwen is out of commission."

"Oh wow." Matt's chagrined.

Gavin turns to me and asks, "Heidi isn't dumb. We caught her doing something good, right?"

"I wish her well," I answer. At first it stunned me to hear her choose the abortion. I was hurting, and I protected myself with sarcasm. I kept calling her "Mother." Now I am silently suffering. I just have the feeling for a minute, until I shake it off. I realize that I got what I wanted. She made the decision.

Heidi may stumble, but I don't want to be the person that makes her fall.

I'm here to help her shine.

Gavin says, "If we are doing anything, it's because we are proud of our school's community. This is a great little show. I'll edit the recording for *Walking and Talking*. I'll play it for Mr. Stace for his approval."

That night I have a dream about Heidi. I went to the city to see her, because CPR needs to be performed on our relationship. "Heidi, we should commit to each other," I say.

She says, "I can't. Neither can you."

Again, a send-away. "You had an abortion. So let's cut the crap."

"So did you. So, no," she says.

"We were made for each other," I say. It's completely sophomoric. I then wake. I stare at the ceiling for a while. Once I become oriented, I change my mind. She didn't pick me, after all. How can we build a relationship on an abortion? I'm not up for grabs this time. Today, I did what I could for Heidi. Honestly, it would be hard for us to advance as a couple.

I'm waiting to graduate from high school. I want to go to college. My parents have died. Nothing is holding me in Centerville. All I have to do now is send out my applications. I could be living anywhere next fall. Finally, I say out loud to myself, "Never mind, I have my own thing."

CHAPTER THIRTY

Heidi

Early in the morning, the bus drops me off at the mall. There is a sales meeting at Übertrends. On the way to the store, I hear, "Hey, Heidi." It's Tina from the kiosk. She waves me over. Tina sells beauty supplies. There are empty boxes all around her. She is stocking her space and says, "I just got this facemask and these moisturizers." She puts them into a bag. I'm interested and hold out a hand. She hands them to me.

"Great. Thanks."

Tina says, "I saw you on the news last night. You'll need that now that you are a celebrity."

I reach into my purse and ask, "Celebrity?"

"Yeah. You don't have to pay me. I've got this one," she says. "When everyone sees how photogenic you are, tell them that you stop by my kiosk."

If Tina saw me on the television, a lot of other people could have as well. It already seems to have had an impact. That must be why that man on the bus thought he recognized me. Also, there was a woman that I don't know who stared at me. I'll make it up to Tina later, but now I've got a meeting.

I say, "Thanks again."

"You have flavor, sister. No doubt."

When I get to the back room, all of the stores employees are there for the meeting. "This is a month-long competition," Sharon says. "We will add up the dollar amount. The person with the most sales wins."

"Do you think you have met the right people?" Cole is walking the room. "Sharon is here to help all of our sales clerks." He sits on the edge of a table. "Übertrends doesn't have a history. I do. While still in high school, I worked as an apprentice at my parents' clothing store." He looks at me. "When I opened up this store at the mall, I tried to sell the same labels. Our Xclothing label is in the news. I know the CEO. We will support him during an investigation."

The group breaks out in confusion. We all look at each other.

"Even when it's hard," Cole says, "I'm willing to stick up for friends."

Sharon, Li, and I step away from the crowd of employees when the meeting ends. Sharon says, "We know—no, make that *everyone* knows—that you are protesting Xclothing."

"It's not like it was confidential, Heidi. It was on Channel 5 news," Li adds.

Sharon balks. "Cole was looking your way the whole meeting."

I know some people walk into this store only to buy Xclothing. I feel challenged. Sharon and I get into a stare down. "The showdown. It's on," I say.

Sharon says, "We'll settle this on the sales floor."

The mall has opened, and a customer comes over to us. I am standing in the middle of the Xclothing section. I'm there to make a little challenge to her. She is eating from a small bag of gummies. The customer says to Li about Xclothing, "I know about the protest, but I love the brand. Besides, some of those kids bring money home to help their families."

It's a lot of style for the price, but I cross my arms. I can only mumble something to her about the protest being important to Übertrends. Then I blurt out about her chewing on THC infused edibles and give her an emphatic "No! I don't think that's how it works."

Sharon ignites. She hisses at me. "I don't want you just standing here for eight hours. Go help the customers."

I walk away with my head held high.

I have been working on a sales technique. Earlier, I helped a man in the jeans section. Now I loom around the dressing rooms. I've set myself up to be of service to him. I tell myself that he will buy something from me before he leaves.

"I need a different cut of pants," I hear him say from the fitting room.

Sharon casually walks by. "He's tried on twenty pairs."

I have all of the discarded pairs in a pile. "I'm bringing him jeans as a favor," I quietly tell her.

He comes out and looks in the mirror. "Oh, okay." I've been working with him for twenty minutes. He's got to buy something. He points and says, "That last pair of jeans that I tried on were a good fit. I'll take them." They are on top of the pile. "Also the jeans I am wearing."

He has changed and brings me the pants. I go for an add-on sale. "Would you like a belt? It's brushed steel."

"Yeah, I like that," he says.

So glad that Übertrends is fully stocked for the holidays. I give him a plastic card with the code letters *JL*. This tag will identify me as the salesperson at the register. I say, "Thanks," as he walks away.

Li has another customer.

"It's the holidays. Buy before everything is picked over."

"A little pushy?" Sharon asks.

"Get them off the fence," Li answers.

When I walk into the back room, Cole is talking to someone that looks familiar. Cole has his back to me. The other guy looks past him. I try to remember how I know this guy. He has his eyes on me. He is patting his stomach and shaking his head. He is giving me a no. He then raises his voice loud enough for it to carry. He says, "Because of what happened earlier."

I recognize him now as the guy I saw on the news last night. He is the CEO of Xclothing. I read the body language and I get the message. He knows that I have ended a pregnancy. They have switched places. I am now looking at the back of the CEO. Cole is looking past him and says loudly, "You'll have to win."

Cole has been friends with the CEO since he worked at his parents' store. He was still in high school. They grew up together. I did not know this until today. I just signed an apartment lease. If I lose this job, I'm not sure how my bills will be paid. I don't think Cole cares what motives I had to join UP. Now I am in a high-stakes bet with him.

When I look at Nolan, he is staring at me. He is conscious of what just happened. He quickly looks away.

Nolan is the only freight handler working at Übertrends. He spends every day in the back room. He works full-time, but he hasn't been keeping pace with the sales clerks. A lot of customers need service. It's the first day of the sales competition. We are already in a rivalry with each other. The clerks have stopped asking him for help. They are now doing his job. It seems like every box has been opened. The stock has been strewn across the table and left on the floor.

"The back room is in chaos," I say. "The brands are not even in the right boxes anymore." I read the invoices to sort some things out. I come across some information. "This invoice says that Xclothing was bought at a discount."

Nolan says, "All of the Xclothing invoices say 'discount.'"

I already think the CEO has trouble with his sustainable outsourcing. His overseas business is with a sweatshop. I wonder if Nolan knows something more about the deal Cole has made. I introduce the subject when I ask, "Did you see Cole talking to the Xclothing CEO?"

He uses his pointer finger to point to his tummy. "That's one hot mess." He winks.

Nolan will not tell me. He is going into my personal business. It's helpless to ask him anything more. I point a finger back at him and shoot out, "Hey!"

The boxes are piled from the floor to the ceiling. They are taking up an entire wall. Cole set up the sales competition as a way to motivate the clerks to sell. He has got a ton of merch, and he has the sales clerks pushing it hard. The winner gets a cash prize.

I was in the middle of a sale. I start to grab anything and go back to the floor. One of the other sales clerks is helping my customer. I couldn't even find what I was looking for in the back. It's lost somewhere in that back room disaster area. I just fold some clothes and put them neatly back onto the shelf.

CHAPTER THIRTY-ONE

Liam

I am alone at my parents' home. New carpet has been installed. The house also got painted. I'm living here until it's sold. I have a minute to catch my breath and think. My allowance comes out of the social security disability checks that are sent. This is something I do not like. It makes me cringe. More pressing is the street fight I have on my hands. Seventy percent of my skin is covered in dry red blotches. I have broken out into a rash.

It's late in the afternoon. I get a phone call from a lady named Mrs. Aiden. She is selling a home alarm with a free monitoring system. It's from a local company. She mentions that she had been working with my mom. I tell her the news. She asks if I am secure. She fact-checks my name and my street. She then asks me if I am well. I tell her I'm fine, but my voice wavers. She tells me she is calling 9-1-1. She is doing it for me. She puts down her phone. I hang on the line. When she returns, she becomes conversational. She asks me if I am alone. She asks for my age. I answer her. I tell her that everything is good. What I am holding is that this lady knows something about the city where I live. She also hears about the people living here. She now knows that I'm alone, and anything else. So I talk to her like we're cousins. I assure her that everything is okay.

I will open an account with a doctor because of my rash. I did not have an appointment scheduled to see one, but it seems like Mrs. Aiden just did that for me. She really has called 9-1-1. I can hear a siren getting close. We end the call. The fire department EMTs knock on my door. I go with them. On the way to the hospital, I tell the tech about the phone call. He says, "A telemarketer? Shoot, that's got to be trinity.

I enter the hospital through the ER. They run tests. They give me a cat scan and a spinal tap. They put me into a bed, start an IV, and pull the curtains shut on their way out. After an hour, I am still in the ER. I am surrounded by a wall of curtains. After two more short hours, a few people come to check on me. "How is everything going?" the ER doctor asks me.

They have been pumping me full of saline solution. That's for sure. The IV they gave me is not mobile. There is not a button to call the nurse. I cannot get to a damn toilet. So I take off my pants and underwear. I tell myself that I don't like being tethered. "I put a number two into the bed," I say with humility.

The bed I'm in is on wheels. They take me upstairs. I'm brought to room 215 and given to a new group of nurses. Everyone at the hospital thinks I am some kind of bedwetter. The nurse wipes my backside. I am put into a new bed. Another nurse comes in to tell me, "There is someone here to see you."

It's my uncle Dan.

"Liam," he says, "I came as soon as I got the call from the hospital. How are you doing?"

I'm in a hospital bed and have an IV in my arm. It looks worse than it is, I think. Grandpa Dean and Uncle Dan are the only people I expected to see during visiting hours. Anyone else would be kind of a surprise. They dragged me into probate court. Everyone there thought putting me on public assistance was a good idea. Everyone but me, but I'm biting my tongue. The public stepped right through that door. I blame the public for the rash.

"Just being cautious," I tell him. "I'm here to have a rash checked."

"Well, tell me what you have been doing. How did you end up here?"

"Really, I'm doing okay. It's only the rash."

"How about your girlfriend?" he asks. "Is that something we can talk about?"

Often, I have Heidi on my mind. Being in the hospital has really kept me busy. I think of her for the first time today. "We aren't going to go any further. We haven't been in touch with each other. Whatever."

"It sounds like you have lost your fighting spirit."

I only thought of abortions as being something that I knew was legal, before this happened. I also thought Heidi could have the procedure and we could get back together. I still liked her. After? People are yakking every time I am out in public. I feel accused of something. Our relationship cannot withstand this kind of study.

"I don't know. It's been really hard to face the music, I guess."

"Look, Grandpa Dean is working hard for you. So you just hang in there. Okay?"

I don't care if people think that allowing the EMTs to take me to the ER was a bad choice. Anyone can see the rash on my arms, belly, and legs. I would like a doctor to take a look. Both of my parents had cancer. I'm scared about my health. Visiting hours are ending, but before Uncle Dan leaves, I tell him, "I'll just get a full examination and there will be no guessing about my health."

Uncle Dan tells me Grandpa Dean will take care of the costs.

After the first twenty-four hours at the hospital, I get some sleep. They start early in the morning with some bloodwork. I order breakfast and eat. After, they take me in a wheelchair to another room for an EKG. Then I'm returned to my room. They continue to run an IV. It's pesky. I am bothered because I think it will ruin all of the tests.

It's around lunchtime, and my sister calls. She goes into a spiel about how she auctioned off some of the items she got from our parents. Mom had a fur coat. Allison tried it on, but the sleeves were above her wrists. It didn't fit. So she sold it to someone. It makes me wonder if we will ever stop turning animals into coats. Fuck fur. Allison has been making other deals at online auctions. At first, she just sold some things. Now she is a buyer. She had a winning bid for an Asian folding partition that she liked.

I don't stay on the phone long because the doctor comes in to talk. He says, "We got the lab work back, and the tests look good. We gave you a few bags of solution. It's time to let it work. We are going to take out the IV and send you home."

When I get home, I go over the discharge instructions. I have been told to make a follow-up appointment as an outpatient. The attending doctor wants me to see another doctor about my skin rash. This is not going too badly. I wasn't flagged on the tests. There is nothing imminent. He has let me out of the hospital.

Mrs. Aiden called on a Wednesday. I missed classes again. I am in the attendance office Monday morning when the principal walks in and says, "You can't just have your friend excuse you. You must have a note."

Principal Eldwood likes to keep watch over the students at Lincoln. He thinks people my age are easily misguided. The staff at Lincoln would like to be there if I committed some offense, I'm sure. When I was at Memorial, the hospital's social worker stopped by my room. She sat down, and we had a talk. She knows about the abortion but doesn't think that it hits on one single profile. She says, "Every day, people from all walks of life must make the choice."

The student aide turns to our principal and says, "He has one."

Principal Eldwood reads the doctor's note he has taken from her. He hands it back and says, "Get a grip, young man."

I go to the front office to get my missed homework. There is a note from my homeroom teacher asking if we could meet. I check the clock on the wall. It's still early enough that we would have a few minutes to talk.

I catch him in the classroom. "Hi, Mr. Soth. I got your note?"

"If I could talk to you, Liam."

I walk up to his desk.

"After the World War, America was stripped of its special wartime powers. The country went back to normal. I happen to be reviewing. You see?"

I missed this lecture because I was in the ER. "Yes," I answer.

"Our country was no longer engaged in a battle against our foes. We had friends across the globe."

"Yes, exactly . . ." Mr. Soth knows about the procedure. I start to tell him that I have to make some of my own choices on diplomacy. I'm just going through a learning curve. I'm beginning to orient myself. Then he cuts me off.

"That didn't last long, though, because of new conflicts. It's war! Understand? War, war, war."

Students start entering the classroom. This time I get the message. I'm sure I am not getting a pardon. Mr. Soth is a passionate man. He has brought me up to speed on his class. With everything, really. I get out a "thanks" and back away from his desk.

Gavin and Seth didn't save me a seat today. I've got one minute before the bell rings. I sit next to Jamie Smilt. Our grandfathers went to law school together. I've known him since elementary school. We talk once or twice during the school year.

"How's life treating you?" I ask.

"You're such a tool." He sneers.

CHAPTER THIRTY-TWO

Heidi

It's the holidays. The mall is mobbed. My lungs feel smooshed, and my breathing has become very shallow. I am on my break. I stop by Tina's kiosk. She puts a Back in Five Minutes sign out. We step outside. We aren't allowed to smoke at the entrance where we are standing, but Tina does. I tell Tina, "If I don't win the competition, these are my last days at Übertrends."

Tina says, "Girl. No way."

We live in a very nice section of the city. "Tina," I say, "I can't even be sure about where I will live."

A rent-a-cop pulls his compact car up to the curb. Tina drops her cigarette and steps on it with her foot. After he passes, she says, "It will be moving day for someone else, sister. You already live the zip code."

UP did not stop the protest. It has been very effective. I am able to register with people. This makes me look pretty good. My *Alpha Cash* audiobook says I have bought myself a second chance. Xclothing hired some lawyers and tried to silence the picketing. The government lawyers were still working the case. The group of lawyers looked into everyone's past.

Cole told me, "People easily forget their lapses, but it's easy to dig up the dirt."

Xclothing was in the news at night. During the day, we all saw Cole in the back nervously trying to talk it out with his bank. A lot was learned from the investigation. Such as, the labor department had already brought their case. The CEO had an early appearance in court. It was as silent as a spider. The CEO did not want to be sitting on what would become last season's clothing. He made a move before everything was leaked out to the media. If Cole would buy from Xclothing in bulk, the CEO said he would discount the price.

There is still more to come. We are all waiting.

Tina is having lunch with me today. I am talking about the people who ask me to do them a favor. I start to go into these generalities about how I always get a certain end result. I do a complete info-dump. I say, "I have mixed feelings about doing whatever, because, you know, it's not fair. Still, I end up doing what everyone asks."

Tina says, "Make a stand, sister. Live to say yes!"

I expect a new set of social rules. Mostly they are unwritten. People have something to hold over me. It's real power. *Alpha Cash* says it can be exchanged for services. Just last month I took on an extra shift for one of the part-time employees. She wanted to go to a hockey game. I agreed. She told me, "You're such a sweetie." Sadly, I was afraid to say no. I didn't want her to get into my personal business. I know how fast that could shut me down. So I played along. Tina is telling me to step into this role. Can saying yes be that bad? Being eaten like sugar is on the top of my list of what I must get over.

When the mall closes to customers, we meet in the back room. Cole and Sharon go over the two-week progress report. The competition is getting good. Everyone has been on edge over the Xclothing protests, but there is some good news. Cole says, "The tumult seems to have attracted new customers into the store." The girls that have started coming into the store are allowing me to dress them up. My sales numbers are climbing.

Sharon says, "We can't keep enough stock on the shelves. We stack it, and it sells."

Cole is going over the sales numbers. He is tight-lipped. If the store is making money, we can only guess. "Look, girls. We have the whole month to think about."

I'm way ahead of you, mister. People saw me on television. I am being asked for by name. By this time, I have sold the "Heidi" brand. I have been collecting names from all of my sales. I have a lot of new contacts. What I hear most often is, "You're a lot taller in person."

I was listening to my *Alpha Cash* audiobook all along. After hearing chapter 5 say that I should be able to find a solution for my problem, I made it a goal. I have been working to get clients. I have met a lot of new people doing volunteer work with UP, and we trade business cards. Some come into the store. It has started my career. The narrator reads at the end of the chapter that I have succeeded in turning the corners in my life.

In the afternoon, Cole is usually in the back room doing the books. Today he is on the sales floor.

I see Li working with a customer. She is around my age.

"I like going to the clubs. What do you have?"

Li shows her some stuff and says, "These are popular, but you'll love the price."

The girl starts picking out tops and bottoms, before realizing that it is Xclothing. The protests have been going on for weeks. The word is out there now.

The girl levels a stare at Li.

Li says, "We've got to fuel the dream any way we can."

The girl puts down all but one of the items. She buys a dress and leaves.

"Seen it done before. You are on your way. Very becoming," Cole tells her.

Sharon clicks her tongue at Cole. She tsks him. He's only trying to keep the competition going, but he turns pink. He must have a lot on his mind. The Xclothing is now leaving the store very slowly. What is left to sell are the more expensive labels. It takes a more experienced clerk to make a sale.

"This looked so, so good on you—amazing even," I say to a customer as I drop her receipt into a bag.

It was a repeat customer of mine, and Sharon says to me, "Tough to find fault with you."

The hours I have out on the sales floor are starting to add up for me in a meaningful way. "What can I say? I wrap them in style."

"It was difficult for me because of the obstacles I had while trying to build this business," Cole says all choked up. "This could be a smooth career path for you, Heidi."

"Lots of good deals," I say with a smile, but wonder, what obstacles?

"I have been here before." A customer just walked into the store. "I am looking for the designer that puts a polyethylene lining into his clothes."

"He's mistaken. That's from our competitor," Cole tells Sharon. "That's just a plastic for weatherproofing." He holds everyone off with a whisper. "I'll take this one."

"Is this for an activity that keeps you outdoors?" Cole is already closing.

"Yes."

Cole shows the man a jacket made from the most durable fabric we sell. "This is what you came in for today. Am I right?"

"Yes."

It's weatherproof and fashion forward. "You just can't leave it behind. Am I right?"

"Yes."

The boss makes a good, clean sale. At the register, the man gives a credit card. He shows his ID. His information is put into our directory. He is one of our customers now.

CHAPTER THIRTY-THREE

Liam

While Allison was home for Mom's funeral she picked a few things to take with her to campus. We also decided on belongings we did not want. It was easy to stick them in the garage. Also, we stored stuff in the basement. Some people from the Humane Army are here to take everything. After a man from the charity loads everything from our house into the truck, I speak to his supervisor. He says, "Just because we are a charity, it doesn't mean we want your ten-speed bike. Just by looking I can see that the tires are flat, the handlebars are bent, and the seat is torn."

I report all of this to Grandpa Dean.

He says, "Even the Humane Army will fight."

I nod. Life has been pushing me around pretty good. I hand over the receipt they wrote for all of the donations.

"I'll take care of the taxes," he says.

I nod.

"Have you gone to the doctor like the hospital recommended?" I'm asked.

It's a gut check. If I was actually sick, I don't think I could go to the doctor. I don't know if I am healthy, either. The medicine they gave me at the hospital has not done the job. My skin rash has not waned. I feel able to get through a doctor's exam. I don't think it would be too much trouble. I play along. "They gave me the name of a doctor. I'll make an appointment."

I am not surprised when Grandpa says, "You will need to fill out some forms." He tells me, "I am conserving the trust." Grandpa will not just dole out money from the trust fund. First, he is going to try to get money out of the government medical plan I am on. If you know how to ask the Medicare PPO insurance people properly, some medical visits are reimbursed.

Everyone in town is chirping about the abortion. Whenever I am confronted, it is always by a person that has become energized. They are always wounding me with their words. I have a chink in the armor. Also, I'm getting in deeper and deeper with the social security office. I don't like the feeling, and I can't take on everyone. People say that we have to pick our fights.

We move on to a new topic. "There has been some progress in your case," he says. "Your parents had several investments. One of them was at Poseidon brokerage. A senior money manager called. He asked me to keep your money at his office. He offered to manage it himself."

Grandpa hands me a portfolio. I look over the pages. Grandpa has put all of my money into this account. It says I am flush with cash. Grandpa has been working with the money for months. He was sullen and churlish after the abortion. Grandpa Dean and Uncle Dan are trying to bring new business into the law firm. I extend the olive branch when I say, "Anything that does emerge because of your management as trustee, you can keep. It's a bonus for you."

After the holidays, things are still uppity. I go to the CPC cemetery. I usually come on a Friday afternoon.

There is a fresh blanket of snow on the ground. I brush off the markers.

My heart is swollen.

I am at the gravesite. There are two markers. I've lost two parents. It has been hard all the way around. As the year has rolled by, I've become more resolved. While grieving, some people go through different stages. There is not a set amount of time this takes. My dad died about three years ago. I've been through the entire process. I'm oriented. I have my health. I've had a quiver in my gut so far, but now the shake in my throat is gone.

My thoughts break off because I hear someone. There is a man about twenty feet away. He is sitting on a bench and looking at me. If I'm out somewhere, it seems like I run into this guy. I want to tell him that everything is good. It's good at school, with Heidi, and with my grandpa Dean. I don't. I may see him around, but he is still a stranger.

I greet him. I say, "Hello."

He nods, but I can't place him.

I make another stop at Udders. I'm there eating a bowl of cereal when Jane walks in with Matt. They both see me. She pulls out the wallet she has in her back pocket and hands Matt some money. He gets into line. This is the first time I have seen her since the abortion. A few things run through my mind as she walks over to my table: (a) she says abortions should be done on demand, and (b) I know that I am about to get an earful.

"Hello," I say.

"Hello yourself."

"How is everything going?" I want to know.

"That's what I should be asking you."

"What?" I ask.

"So? How is our hellcat?"

Jane is asking me about Heidi. I answer her, saying, "I wouldn't know."

Jane says, "I've heard about your little mistake. I know everything."

Great. "I've learned something, Jane. Okay?"

Jane has more. "I'm okay with girls getting together with boys, Liam. It's just that everyone has to play nice."

I guess that's fair. "We were able to shake hands after," I tell her.

She looks for Matt before saying, "Fuck you both, Liam." It's like she is talking for every girl in the world. When I went to Lincoln's media center, Gavin told me that the drama department had rebuffed Heidi. They won't display any pictures if she is in them. I have been held up in court. We have both hit the wall. Matt has made his order to go. "I've gotta go. Good chat," Jane says as Matt makes his way over to my table. She intercepts him. He waves from a distance as he is swept out the door.

Heidi

The media drowned the Xclothing CEO in a sea of words. Eventually, the court ordered the company to pay a steep fine. The whole time, the CEO denied knowledge of a sweatshop. To close the case, he had to apologize. Then he was shut down. Later, the government put new taxes and regulations on small business's working overseas. A government spokesperson came forward to call the action a success. He said, "If we want our country to be the best, everyone has to do their part."

All of the lawyers went into overdrive. Lance Knupp has a police record from when he was younger. During a protest he broke a window. He used spray paint to leave a message. "Sure, I really take it to them," he said. Our call to protest Xclothing falls apart under the scrutiny. The UP website was ordered to be taken down. There weren't any more donations. The not-for-profit could no longer pay rent.

"I have to say that the lawyers won," Curt says. "I know who got paid, and it was the lawyers." There is a banker box full of files he covers with a top.

Jean-Pierre says, "We closed the sweatshop. Still, they think their oppression will disillusion us."

UP did some good work, but we've been warned. I wonder if this group will take things any farther. I start to sweat.

Lance reads me. "Just remember to do good."

Kyle hands Lance a printout and says, "On to the next spot. On to the next protest."

It's the last day of the sales competition. Sharon is holding a clipboard as I walk into the store. As usual Li's mom has gotten her to work on time. I'm running about ten minutes late because the bus route has a lot of delays.

She looks at her watch and writes something down. I'm one of the four girls that are full time. I'm not in too deep. I've worked all of my shifts this month. The other sales clerks have not.

Li breaks the ice with a customer, "Hey, I know you from school."

"You're a Stinger?" the girl asks Li.

"Absolutely." Li smiles. "Aren't you a senior?"

"A junior, actually."

I smile at Li. She can have her twenty hours a week. We were never in competition with each other. Actually, I've been getting a lot more shit from Sharon. In the afternoon, some new business comes my way. During the last hour of the sales competition, I spend my time thrilling the customer with the more expensive labels. The sale falls through.

At the end of our shift, we stay on the sales floor. Not everyone is here, but we have a quick meeting. Sharon is going to tell us who the standouts were this month. She says, "Okay. In punctuality? It's Li. For schedule adherence? It's Heidi."

Cole holds two fingers to his head and salutes.

While looking at Li, Sharon says, "We got some returns." She looks out at everyone and says, "Overall sales numbers were good. The best sales clerk in this competition is Heidi." Everyone claps. "Okay," says Sharon, "I'm going to get a picture. I'll post it. Everyone will know that the results are in and the competition is over."

I stand under one of the store's neon signs. Sharon focuses her phone camera on me. My face and body soak up the hazy blue-and-pink light. She snaps the picture. It's complete bliss. Xclothing is no longer outsourcing with a company using child labor. I won the competition. I am the best salesperson in the store. My precarious situation with Cole is over.

Cole says, "I'm very happy to see you in the winner's circle."

Cole lost the CEO as a partner but said no more than, "That's the cost of doing business." I start to see the Übertrends story. The CEO was definitely a dark chapter. Then I look at Cole. He has driven the same car for the last eight years. He lives alone at a nearby apartment complex. Yet I see the clothes in his store sell really well. He has a tight grip on the reins—if he is much of a success. Cole was never a part of the investigation that the government made. I don't think he knew the deal he made with the CEO was tainted. I think he was innocent. Contrastingly, he looks to me to be more of a fat cat every day.

"It's hard work," I say to everyone. "It was worth the effort."

We go in the evening to a chain restaurant in the mall. The stores close at nine but the restaurant stays open late. All of the female salesclerks are in cocktail dresses. Nolan, the guy from freight, doesn't look bad either. A few of the salespeople from other stores in the mall have been watching since we entered. I won the sales competition. I'm taken tonight to celebrate. We have sort of grouped together. No one is talking. We are just holding our drinks.

Li breaks the silence when she says, "I know what it's about, and it only works if you are one of the super-elite kids."

Whenever I mingle with Li, I can be sure where she will take the conversation. She does not hold the abortion against me the way some other people do. She has her own mind. It doesn't pour out of her like a poison. She doesn't call it out to seize me. It's not an ongoing battery. In fact, she just called me elite.

I snicker.

We know the chef at the restaurant. After explaining we are celebrating, they send over drinks. My drink is called a sugar blue and served in a martini glass. I asked them if they could set it on fire, but I know it was made without the alcohol.

A sales person we know from the national department store in our mall says to me, "congrats, slut."

We hear her tell her friends something about Tina. "She's kinda dumb."

Then they inform us that Nolan is our lush. "No wait," she says. "I mean your chimney."

Our little group gets what transgressions we've made. We are in on the joke. All at once all say "to a league of our own."

We clink our glasses.

Sharon comes down to the party. I hear her pitch in "poor things." She's talking to the girls trolling us. She walks toward me and then gestures with her head. We step away from everybody and close to the wall. "I have watched that man for the last nine years," she says. "He leaves early to go on a date. After a night of partying, he comes into work around noon. Not me. I'm there. It's not hard to find me. I take his calls. When he can't be found, I listen to the girls' cry. So they talk. Heidi, do you know what the word misogynist means?"

"I don't know. It doesn't sound very nice."

"Just as you say, Heidi. And I'm stuck here."

I assume what Sharon just told me happened years before I got to Übertrends. No secrets among friends, I guess. I know that Cole is in the store every day. He works hard. I see him working the phones, going over the books, and dealing with customers. Sharon might know where he has been in the past, but I can't think of any time I was in the store when he wasn't there working.

Sharon goes back to the store.

She works insane hours.

I look for my most inner voice. I find the *cashier*. Let the trolls bring their stuff. For example, they call me an "abortion." One of their boys holds out an arm and moves it back and forth. He makes a vroom, vroom noise. They say, "You got vacuumed." At this point I process their words. They come at me like a product with a barcode. I imagine scanning the package of words and hearing a beep. LED numbers light up on the register. In my head the *cashier* is

239

using a free hand to push the keys clickety-clack. I make small change:

"We're better than beasts," I say with some authority.

I hide to get the troll's real stories. I listen in on everyone. This one here steals office supplies from her boss. The one over there sold a car. I hear that it's a real lemon. I've been at the till all night. *Alpha Cash* says that I'm filling the register drawer.

CHAPTER THIRTY-FIVE

Liam

Grandpa passes the word he got from the social security office down to me. He says, "Whether you are walking around or out cold, you are covered with a government medical plan."

I have an office visit scheduled for today. A nurse walks me to an examination room. She wants me to change into a gown before the doctor comes into the room. At the ER, several doctors have already seen the rash. This is the new doctor. It's the first time I have been to an internist. When the doctor comes into the room I tell him, "I had a doctor, but he was called a pediatrician."

The internist is sixty, holding a computer pad, and typing in some notes. "That's for babies. You're a young man," he says.

When I was in the hospital, the ER doctor put me through a lot of tests. I gave the internist access to those medical records. "I was at the ER. Did you look at all of the pictures and samples that were taken?"

The internist says yes. He knows that I have a rash. It is the focus of today's examination. He looks me over. The gown is open in the back, and my legs are sticking out. Most of the rash is still visible. It is stubbornly on me. He shakes his head and says, "It doesn't look good."

He has the results from the hospital visit that I had, but I put myself over to him once more. "I've had an abortion," I meekly confide.

"Your halcyon days are over." He howls with laughs.

"Is there a diagnosis? Can I have the summary?"

"You are sick."

I shuttle about every day. During the week, I have school. Also, I can call my friends. When the weekend comes I pick up groceries, do my banking, and put gas in the car. I am feeling good. I am healthy.

On paper? Not so much.

"I'm living a double life," I quip.

He rolls me over to my side and puts on a rubber glove. The internist says, "We all have an inch." He inserts his thumb into my anus. "A way to bounce off the blows from the harsh world. It's a very efficient invisible shield. It's made up of our thoughts and feelings. When there is a probe that punctures these protective powers, we get crazed."

I go back to the beginning. Once I began collecting disability money from the social security office the public came out of the woodwork. I began to notice these red splotches. After telling me that I am free to go, the doctor leaves the room. He did this exploration on my body, but I was expecting a medical remedy. Why didn't he prescribe a balm I could slather onto my body? Perhaps a skin cream might work. I get dressed quickly and exit. I walk down the hall. I don't look into any of the rooms. I want to just leave the office without talking to anyone, but I am stopped at the desk. The lady has called my name. She wants me to make an appointment.

I should be ready to explode, but that isn't the case. Today's appointment may not have gone too well. I am a little confused about the doctor's method, but I believe I will be able to make a quick recovery. In twenty minutes I'll be good as new.

I lie to her. "I need to check on the date. I'll call."

I'm in the car and down the street. Today's office visit was only a body blow. I remind myself that I have had some real challenges. While my parents were sick, I had too many shortcomings. At first, I wasn't able to help them. The relationship I had with my girlfriend wasn't a success. I have to work out an abortion. Overall, I have faced more, like when I spent some time in jail.

I am thinking all of this will toughen my hide.

Gavin, Seth, and I went to Udders. We all sat down at a table. I ordered and am eating from my birthday cake bowl. Seth says, "This is your eighteenth birthday. I picked something special out for the occasion." He lays out three scratcher cards. The kind where you have to match a picture, or find numbers. I become a little uneasy and suck my smoothy through a straw.

Seth says, "A player could win cash and prizes."

Gavin puts a heaping spoonful of cinnamon cereal into his mouth. He is still chewing when he spits out, "Those cards are entertaining as hell."

After seeing the present, I can only think this is bedlam. I feel I am between a rock and a hard place. The court has expectations. So do my friends. I don't know if I can win. Yet I am eighteen today. I have more available knowledge to make a good choice. I half expect someone to nab me. I ask myself if this could end in handcuffs? Fully awake I look up to see if anyone is onto us. I see Gavin pull the cards to him. He looks at them. Then he slides them back and asks, "Which one are you going to play first?"

While I pretend to look them over, I buy some time to think. I am only going to play the three tickets. I'm sure that doesn't require counseling. Don't school's benefit from these purchases? I doubt that there is a person who would actually come forward to condemn me. There just aren't enough hours in a day. Even Judge Cannow won't have the time.

The first card I scratch off has an image of a professor named Archeologist Albert. I find three spears and read that the card will pay out thirty-five dollars.

Seth says, "You are a winner."

After all I have been through, I don't want to miss out on anything. I scratch the other tickets, but this time I lose twice. Still, I think that I was smooth. Everything went pretty well.

I say, "Yep. A win. Three spears."

Gavin says, "Yeah. Look, you won. It's been a million miles of fun."

CHAPTER THIRTY-SIX

Heidi

It's early in the afternoon and I am at Übertrends. I am sorting the mail. I hold onto a letter a charity has sent. I give the rest of the mail to Nolan. Li walks up to the counter. Cole and Sharon are in the back.

During the sales competition, Sharon and I locked horns more than once. Sharon may get catty, but she comes first. I have been able to put others before myself. I have done this with some success. Like the time I worked a shift for one of our part-time girls. The extra hours have helped me gain the sales experience I need. In this spirit, I am going to help out our boss. It's not much. I'm only thinking that he can tick off *Girl* in his weekend file.

I say to them, "I've noticed that Sharon has something for Cole."

Nolan says, "She has been chasing him down from behind for years."

Li alerts us all, "She better catch him soon. She's already an old maid."

I leave them with my final thought: "I'm sure the two of them would make a good couple."

Sharon is embarrassed about the admission she made at the restaurant. She told me that Cole is a womanizer. She feels like it was a meltdown and has been apologizing to me all day. She is ready to do anything to put it in her past. I think of a certain something we could do with Tina. No one says it out loud, but we all think it will help her get Cole. Tina from the kiosk is a talented cosmetologist. She could turn back the years on Sharon's clock. A few years at least. Sharon is ready to make nice. I sell a spa day with the girls. Sharon agrees to a makeover.

Several months have gone by since the ER doctor told me to have my eyes checked. I had medical insurance. I didn't have the supplemental plan. I have never been to an eye doctor. When I look out, I see a world that is fuzzy. My eyesight has been neglected. I can't ignore another year. I have saved some money. I also have the prize money from the sales contest. I am going to use it to fix my eyes. I do some research on laser surgery. I find a surgeon, because he advertises himself on television. Actual clients give their testimonials. They talk about how easy the surgery was, and how their vision has been corrected. After each client speaks, the doctor comes onto the screen. He uses the catchphrase, "Be spot-on, without the specs."

At the surgeon's office, I fill out a booklet given to me. It asks questions like, "Do you ever overlook objects and then hit them with your body?"

I answer yes.

The surgeon then gives me an eye exam and says, "You have an ordinary condition called hyperopia." I ask if I could set up an appointment, and the doctor agrees to take me as a patient. I will have my eyes lasered. The next week I'm scheduled for the surgery. While I am in his operating room, they clamp my eyes wide open. One at a time. The laser is focused on each eye for about five seconds. The doctor is shaping my corneas. When the surgery is completed, I sit up.

"My eyes sting," I say.

The doctor puts his finger under my chin and tilts my head back. He gives me eye drops and says, "The medicine will act like your natural tears. I will give you the bottle to take home. It's important that you follow a regimen. I don't want your eyes to dry out."

"The light is blinding," I say.

"Your eyes are dilated." The surgeon pushes a pair of glasses onto my face. "These will keep out the bright light. Wear the glasses for the rest of the day, and again if there is more sensitivity. Only take them off when you are ready to sleep."

"Yes."

"I need you back here in ten days to monitor your recovery."

At the apartment, I lie down on my bed. I sleep and I dream. I am on a shift at Übertrends. I am the only clerk working. It's late morning, and the store is busy with customers. I step out from the back room and onto the sales floor. I am wearing my costume from *Weekdays the Musical*. My suit coat stops at my waist. I'm wearing a mini skirt. I have on red patent leather knee-high boots. All of the customers rush directly to me. They group together in front of me. One of them says, "I saw you in an advertisement and I didn't think you actually work at the store."

I nod vigorously and answer, "My real name is Heidi. This is my real job."

Another customer says, "This is fantastic. Your advertising really hooked me."

Cole is full of sunshine. He walks up and asks everybody, "Isn't it a great day?"

"The best," I answer.

Cole says, "Heidi. Everybody. Come with me. I have something to show you."

I go with Cole, and the cluster of customers follows. We get to the bathroom door, and Cole puts his hand on the doorknob. He turns it, and the door swings open. It's dark inside. Cole reaches for the light switch on the wall and says, "I really think you are going to like this."

When the lights go on, it's really bright. I step past him. Into the bathroom. Cole has had someone put lights around the mirror. There must be a hundred bulbs. There is a makeup counter. The chair has a wire body and a purple velvet seat. It's a lady's vanity room.

He says, "You are my sales star. I did it for you."

A customer says, "She's a celebrity. A genuine celebrity."

After the eye surgery, I return to my job at Übertrends. I show Cole a note from the doctor. It explains that I am recovering from surgery. To protect my eyes, the surgeon gave me a thick oversized rectangular black frame to wear. I tell Cole, "My eyes are still adjusting to the light." He gives me the green light. I am allowed to work. I will be wearing glasses with dark lenses indoors. I suspect there will be a lot of jokes about letting this celebrity business go to my head.

The morning went along without a snag. In the afternoon, Nolan comes up to the counter to get the mail. He pretends not to know me. "Are you new here?" he asks.

"No," I answer quizzically.

"It looks like you are wearing the black bar that censors use. In pictures they place them over a person's eyes so they can't be identified."

Anyone in the mall can identify me. I get trolled every day. After the abortion, I sometimes want to run and hide from people. I try to play it down. "What?" I ask.

Cole has hired a new full-time employee. His name is Evan. "Abby, abby, abby," he says breathlessly. "I know that it's you!"

I hold up three fingers and tell him, "Read between the lines."

Nolan brings a fine point to the exchange. "You can't just trick us with the glasses. You have a reputation."

There is no inflation in my life. Just when I think things are taking shape something will come along to make me feel flat. This time it hits home. My arms are hanging at my sides, but I clench my hands into two fists. I grunt and I scream out, "I am cursed."

Li and all of the other clerks stop what they are doing. Everyone is looking at me.

I am totally frustrated.

I bite my bottom lip.

At the follow-up appointment, the eye surgeon tells me the healing is ahead of schedule. He tests me. He asks me to read some charts and says, "The hyperopia is corrected."

"What does that mean for me?" I ask.

"From now on, you will be seeing the world with twenty-twenty vision," he answers.

When I get home, I remember that I told Mom I would call her. She knew I had a surgery scheduled. I get her on the phone. I let her know that I had the eye surgery. I tell her, "It worked out better than I expected."

Mom says, "I'm so happy for you."

Then I say a few things about my job. I tell her that I could no longer find the fun at work.

Mom says, "Abortions are expensive. You have paid the price."

CHAPTER THIRTY-SEVEN

Liam

We are going back to address the court. The judge has been running my case like it's a serial. He learns something new about me each time I am in court. Grandpa has been acting as the trustee. The paper chase is still relentless. All of my doctor appointments, the various receipts of purchased goods, and the paperwork from the ad litem's office are being collected. Everything is copied, and sent to the court. My file is heavy. If it were dropped, it would fall through the floor.

When I get into the courtroom, rim baldy waves me over to him. He is sitting in the back of the courtroom. On the last bench. After I sit down, he opens up a folder. We huddle together.

He softly says, "Liam, I have been listening to you."

After Judge Cannow stepped into the picture I pulled my punches. I've taken a seat to everyone. Although, when I look at the court, I can see that they are acting like the Hero.

I started to collect social security checks, because the judge wanted to tighten his grip on me. That's when the public really came forward. They question me. At one point, I thought I could ignore them. Now I answer them each time. Our congressmen want to know what their constituents think. The court facilitates this event.

The judge says, "We are going to have our peace."

I have capitulated.

Rim baldy continues, "The court understands that the actions taken have been a pain to you."

"It's more than the court. Everything has spilled out onto the streets."

"Yes, the public has been turning over the abortion issue. That is why the court asked the Social Security Administration to send you public assistance. The judge is redressing your participation in this case."

There is always a group of people. They try to put me in my place. I shout back. We've got to let people know where we stand. Anyway, I am starting to see a bigger picture. I can't let abortion be banned. I have shouldered the problem. I am now a part of the fight for our rights.

A few minutes later my case is called. We walk to the front of the room. It's back to work. "Well," the judge asks, "what have you been up to, Mr. Dean?"

"The money has been collected. I have secured the asset," Grandpa answers.

Judge Cannow looks over the financial statement from Poseidon. He says, "I have reviewed the books. Everything is in order. Mr. Dean is an adequate proxy." Then he asks, "How are you, Liam?"

Judge Cannow has gotten a close look at Grandpa. I think he has been examining both of us. All of this started when Grandpa Dean used the court to set up a trust. The last time I complained, the court took it and ran. I didn't want the checks. They thought I had hung a huge Help Wanted sign out. All of us ended up in court with each other. I do not want to raise any red flags.

"Pretty good," I say.

"Good, good," he says. Judge Cannow taps his gavel and smiles at us. Nothing has changed, but we are done for the day.

My wagon is hitched to Grandpa's star.

CHAPTER THIRTY-EIGHT

Heidi

Iam at the Lincoln theater reunion. I am looking into a showcase at a blown-up picture of the cast of our musical. It was our first dress rehearsal, and I am front and center. The girl stays in the picture. I look away to scan the room. It's a good turnout. At least fifty people are already here. Everyone is gravitating toward the people that have been a part of their plays. I see Mr. Stace and his retinue. They are floating from one group to the next.

"Heidi?" I hear someone call my name. I look back, and I see Rob Aulk. "Heidi. It's so good to see you," he says. Rob had a lot of lines with me. We were together a lot on the stage for rehearsal. He was the male lead in the musical. He asks, "And who are you with?"

Eve has been standing quietly next to me. I introduce him to Rob. I look away from them and, again, into the showcase. They spin around, and Rob laughs. He says, "Great picture. Do you remember that, Heidi?"

"Yeah."

Rob turns to Eve and asks, "Do you know who that is?"

Potted plants come and go. This is a picture of me sitting in a chair. The other cast members are standing behind me. Eve tilts his head and looks intensely at the picture. "It's a princess," he says, "but she's not spoiled."

I'm not spoiled, rancid, and sour? I can really reach Eve. He remembered when I summarized the musical to him. I smile at him. Then I rotate to see who has walked over since we first came into the room. Our full cast is here. Everyone is greeting each other and sharing memories. I see Bailey talking to Mr. Stace. Standing behind them is Dominic. When I look at him, he shakes his head vehemently no, but he is just another car in the train coming at me.

Mr. Stace makes his way over to me. Everyone turns toward us. He takes my hand in both of his and says, "I saw some of your work."

I was able to stop the bad business Xclothing was doing with Cole. I feel proud. "No one wants to play second banana to a CEO that cheats, Mr. Stace."

"Yes. It's heartwarming," he says. "Your campaign with UP is something to be admired."

We all focus on Dominic. He looks like he is about to say something, but he just can't pinpoint what. He nods and smiles.

It's a small consolation.

Mr. Stace says, "Well, we are all lucky to have you." He lets go of my hand and walks over to the next group.

I still have everyone's attention when Rob says, "It was incredible when I saw you on *Walking and Talking*. How is everything going?"

Lincoln High School has a popular show. People really are watching. "Great. Yeah. That went great," I say. "These days I'm more charity and a lot less protest."

A few people laugh. Then everyone goes back to their own conversations.

Bailey comes over and asks, "What have you been up to, Eve?"

"He had a phone interview with the president of a national hotel chain," I answer. "He won't be going back to the park. He landed a new job."

I have given her the right information. Eve nods his head to confirm.

Bailey says, "We'll miss you." She sounds sincere.

Eve has an older brother named Sam. He has special needs. The older brother would play tricks on Eve. Sometimes he would cross the line. One time he ate Eve's goldfish. This is when they were little, little. Eve screamed. He was wailing. He was sensitive to his brother. He didn't know why he would eat his pet. His mother came to ask about the situation. Sam had a speech disorder. It was hard to understand what happened for a while. Sam's explanation was not coherent, until he finally said in deep and gutsy voice, "Then we're even."

The older brother had something special to share with Eve. Eve is a tolerant person. He proved that to me when he found out that I had the abortion. Everyone at the park will remember him. He not only played a good guy in a western-style show, but also that is how he plays it in real life. Eve knows when it is time to step up his game. He is there when it counts. Like the time he rescued me at the park meet and greet. There was a bad guy in a squirrel suit hitting on me. Eve turned him away.

"What was the offer?" Ron asks about the job.

"I am being trained to manage one of the hotels," he says, then turns to me. "Heidi is invited to come and live with me."

Everyone looks at me, and I shake my head. I already told him no. Eve is moving to another state. I have fallen for him and wish it wasn't true. Still, I can't cave into him. I built a business. It's pretty. I'm not willing to leave it behind.

Eve adds, "I got hosed."

I change the subject when I ask, "So what's up with you, Bailey?"

Bailey says, "Ron's in a rockin' band. I have put hundreds of miles on my car driving to

the city to see his shows."

"We play out around the city," Ron confirms.

Rae orbits us. "I saw the band. Ron is really good."

Bailey says, "He was always a theater guy."

I nod in agreement. She is talking about his arts and entertainment side. Ron's hair is long. He plays a bass. He looks and acts the rock star part. I say, "We all live in the city. We should go see them play some time."

CHAPTER THIRTY-NINE

Liam

Dear admission counselor,

My dad died when I was thirteen. I have been on the school academic honor roll for three years. It was my family life that left me with so many questions. I had a problem and it wasn't academic. I needed a man. Dad wasn't there for me. I didn't hear his voice. I needed answers but I couldn't sound out what he would say to me.

Dad was a lab researcher. Mom gave me his notes after I was part of a terminated pregnancy. After running tests, he would write small summaries. I went through his journals. He researched the designs of products. Wrote about suggested safety features. His ethics for throwing a service out to the public were down. I broke the code. I had found him. He left behind all of his time, love, and energy. There is real healing power in his words.

I could follow in my dad's footsteps. I would like to be in a lab coat. Like my father. Working on problems that could save a person. Releasing a product that could change a life for the better. Plotting out test results on charts and graphs. Publishing all of my work. Protecting the public. Helping people. That is what I like. I want to be a future lab researcher. Helping all of the people.

Thank you for your consideration,
Liam Dean

CHAPTER FORTY

Liam

All of my senior-year test results have been down. It's been a mix of mostly Bs and a C this semester. I liked my American history class. Mr. Soth has been giving me As. I am meeting with Mr. Herald. I now have a written personal essay to show him.

I asked Mr. Herald if he would give me a recommendation. I need this paper for my college applications. He says, "Whoa, Liam. You hit the nail on the head. There will not be any late discoveries at the college admissions office. Once you find your audience, there will be no misgivings from anyone involved. After reading your essay, I will write the paper you want. You have been a good example. I've gone over the whole record. You have done a good job in and out of the classroom."

I remember when I had to talk to Mr. Herald about losing my father. Later I told him about the abortion. I really got the brunt of it all. He let it out to the rest of the staff at Lincoln. I always went to him though. With his help, I'll get into college.

Today, I thank him.

He sits back in his chair and puts his clasped hands onto the back of his head. "I know it has been hard work, but it has put you on the path to a happy ending."

The snow is gone, and the ground is starting to thaw. It has become spring, and all of the days are longer. Allison talked to Grandpa Dean yesterday. She called to tell him the date of her graduation ceremony. What she has been up to has gotten back to me. I heard that she has fanned out since the last time we talked. She is graduating from college. She has sent her resume out to several auction houses. I remember her wrapping the pottery mom made in paper. She wanted to decorate her on campus apartment with the pyramid. I think of how she made out with everything Mom left for her. I am sure she should be able to make a good living.

Allison told my grandfather, "There is an industry, and it's thriving."

Grandpa Dean agrees with her. He tells her what he knows. "Online auction houses have had undeniable success," he says.

Uncle Dan tells us, "I just saw a billionaire in the news. He paid a record price for a painting."

I've been following the mom and dad. They want a ban on all of the abortion procedures. A band has formed around them. All are asking our state representative for the same. He has crafted a paper that may become an abortion ban law. It looks like they have the momentum. This piece of legislation is being forwarded through Congress. All they need now are the signatures.

Personally, I feel alienated by the public. I have not been getting a lot of respect. People still call me out. I use my voice. All I can do is stand and deliver. Still, I try to get a pass when people find out about the abortion.

I'm worthy, I think.

CHAPTER FORTY-ONE

Heidi

Sharon walks up to me and says, "Heidi, you have been a stellar salesgirl."

Cole is with her. "Übertrends is part of a charity catwalk," he tells me.

Sharon asks me if I would like to "Do some modeling?"

A couple of weeks later we are at a convention center right here in the city. The Federal Trade Commission had a list of stores victimized by the Xclothing CEO. Without being informed we supported child labor. Now we have ganged together. We want a new balance. The labels that we sell have been told that we are working with a charity that helps clothe teens. The group collected donations from the designers that responded. We are going to showcase their work today.

Cole gives me a room card. We are sleeping here. Overnight, I go from being the face of the protest to the voice of the cause. When we are backstage Cole says, "People want to watch your runway walk." It's been a while since I was on a stage. I eventually step out from behind the curtain. The MC tells everyone about the wide bottom pants that I'm wearing. I am focused on my stride but the lighting is a hazard for my walk. I perspire a little. Still I am told that I "Glide over the walk like I am on ice."

Paid freelancers are creating an electronic media campaign. Everything we do here will be on our social media pages by tomorrow. It's the clothes that are the real stars. We have brought in a small crowd. People ask what labels we are wearing. The MC sells everything, until the show has concluded. Then I'm off the stage.

Earlier in the day it was Sharon, Li, and I together. When she can, Tina has a gig at her aunt's spa. We met her there. We signed Sharon up for a full package. A couple of hours later we left. Sharon looks fresh. She looks her best. It has captured Cole. She had his full attention during the show.

We didn't even stop for lunch, but the afternoon is gone. We temporarily break up. Everyone goes back to their rooms to get ready for tonight. After I freshen up, I check my watch. It's seven o'clock. I leave my room for dinner.

Cole has something to give to the "troubled" teens. He is going to clothe them. He is working with Robin Ligg. She runs the charity. Cole gave me a job. I am making a career for myself. Now Cole wants to help move barriers for teens. It's all so redeeming. Cole put boxes onto a dolly. He brought them down to the center's restaurant and set up a display. The boxes are filled with more clothes. We are going to hand some out tonight. A bunch of teens come close to me. I notice that they are very well dressed. We gather around. A camera man gets a picture of us.

The camera man says, "I got what I needed."

We all cheer.

It's late by the time I am walking back to my room. When I get into my hall, I can see a couple kissing in front of their door. They don't notice me. I realize it's Cole and Sharon. I dash into the ice machine conclave. When I peek around the corner, I see Cole open his door. Sharon follows him inside.

Cole is in joy over the store. Sharon's smile has been wide. The success of the sales competition meant a lot to both of them. On the trip to the convention center, I saw them have fun together. They are a pretty good team and share a love for the business. Their relationship is apparent now. Even the part-time salesclerks know what's going on.

Li and I are at the desk. Nolan comes to get the mail.

Li says, "Talk about something being right under your nose."

"Anyone can see a budding romance," I say.

Nolan says, "Cole finally noticed her."

My electronic print campaign with the Übertrends charity has come to an end. I think of Eve living the dream hundreds of miles away. I decide to make a move of my own. I've been searching online websites that have a classified section. I want to move on to sell big-ticket items.

Sharon is engaged to Cole. I knew it could happen. All Sharon needed was this girl to step in and give her a little extra help. I give Cole my two-week notice. I tell him about an interview I have coming up at a car dealership. He tells me to use him as a referral. Cole knows how to get to the dealer. He says to me, "I'll be in to buy a car."

After sending a resume, I have set an interview time with Quality Auto. I feel like my shot at the job is as good as the next girl's. Then, I am called into an office. I am going to interview with the boss. He is watching paper shoot out of a printer, and gestures for me to sit down. I look around. On the wall, he has several plaques. One of them reads A Million Dollars in Sales. His credenza is a shelf for a tall stack of assorted books with "how to sell yourself" titles. He begins when he says sheepishly, "Lots of word of mouth in this business."

Nolan says that I won the sales competition by a nose. Still, I won. I may have had only a few more customers, but they put me over the top. *Alpha Cash* says that my source is like a money tree. I know the interviewer is using a ploy. This guy is a wolf. Perfect. I tell him, "I have almost a dozen clients. You can call any of them for a reference." This got his attention. I go on to answer how I built my platform. I talk about volunteering. I tell him about the business cards I've traded.

"That is a textbook example of how networking is done. The best prospects are the people who already know you. You really have something. I pay all of my employees to make sales. Are you ready to live on commission?"

I say, "Yes."

CHAPTER FORTY-TWO

Liam

Cathy Smith introduces herself to the Tenth Judicial Circuit Court. She is an executive with the Social Security Administration in my state. She is in court with the stranger that has been showing up wherever I go. He has become a familiar face. His name is Pete Elvel. I just learned that he is also from the social security office. He has been a part of an independent investigation run on my case.

Sometime over this year, I heard a justice from one of our high courts describe abortions. She said, "They're all the same. In any and every case, a girl could get an abortion in state up to twenty-four weeks." A mom and dad in our state want to change the current abortion laws. Our state representative has come up with a "pulse petition." Very early in the pregnancy—as early as the sixth week—an abortion could become illegal. Specifically, as soon as a heartbeat can be detected. It's an inch away from a total ban.

Pete Elvel says to the court, "After the procedure, the court was quick to reach out to Liam. He is collecting social security disability checks. During this time, the taxpaying public is on the hook to pay Liam's bills. When this got out, there was a public thirst. Lots of us know that the pulse petition is up for a vote in Congress. People began talking at restaurants, the grocery store, at banks, and at the park."

Pete looks at the judge. "I have all of the testimonials in a report that I have brought with me today. Here's the rundown:"

"Amy Perry, Centerville's librarian, says that, where it is scandalous, it's also redeemable."

"Our Lincoln High School principal, Mr. Eldwood, calls it 'the morning edition.' He says, 'I don't think it's the kind of offense where you should lose your future.'"

"The court ad litem made some comments that I'll read. 'I have observed Liam at different times, and in lots of situations. Liam is a lion only on paper.'"

The public has been as steady as a doctor's hand. I have been compelled to argue my case. Also, the mom and dad got their case heard. My work didn't leave the county. The mom and dad had the ears of our whole state. The results are in now. The pulse petition the mom and dad endorsed will not become law. The congressional vote was more nay.

"He can have it," says the ad litem in a forked tongue. He is talking about the court allowing the legal procedure, or handing out more public assistance. The judge must pick.

There is a real conflict for Judge Cannow. The Social Security Administration has read the opinion he has written. It would suggest that the court was conservative to the right. Now there is a general consensus. Judge Cannow says, "The courts try to uphold our laws, but we are indebted to the people speaking out. They have been our real watchdog." He looks down at the gavel he spins in his hand, and talks into the microphone.

"Take the hard-won knowledge to the top."

The gavel is struck. The courtroom fills with voices.

The court asked that disability checks be sent to me. After everything passed through congress, the social security office reviewed the case. Cathy and Pete were brought into the court today prepared to decline the order, but the judge dismissed the case.

Someone walking past my grandpa says without stopping, "No more social security checks. Sorry."

I win.

I look over at the other table and see Grandpa Dean smiling at me. I have passed the examination. My name is cleared. The public has saved the "patient." No more accusations. It won't end there, because the gag is off. Other people could easily be on good terms with me. The court says so.

ACKNOWLEDGMENTS

You can go to www.CDC.gov to learn of impactful statistics.

Jason Alpert is the author of *Liam and Heidi*.

www.jasonalpert.com